Kelly

CHURCH

Ed Adams

First published in Great Britain in 2024 by firstelement

Directed by thesixtwenty

10 9 8 7 6 5 4 3

A CIP catalogue record for this book is available from the British Library.

ISBN 13: 978-1-913818-47-0
eBook ISBN: 978-1-913818-48-7

Printed and bound in Great Britain by Ingram Spark

rashbre
an imprint of firstelement.co.uk
rashbre@mac.com

ed-adams.net

Thanks

A big thank you for the tolerance and bemused support from all of those around me. To those who know when it is time to say, "step away from the keyboard!" and to those who don't.

To Julie for continued understanding.
To John, for hangin' in there
To Georgina, Caroline, Rosemary, and Angie for cover reviews
To thesixtwenty.co.uk for direction.
To the NaNoWriMo gang for the continued encouragement.
To those who provided inspiration at SPS London 2023.
To the London hotel which gave me a wonderful free room.
To Topsham, for being lovely.
To the edge-walkers. They know who they are.
To a certain Reverend.

And, to a few websites:

Ed Adams Amazon Page:
https://amzn.to/3NRPqXV

Ed Adams Catalogues:
https://ed-adams.net
https://ed-adams.mysites.io

Rashbre blog:
https://rashbre2.blogspot.com

Plus, the cast of amazing and varied readers whether human, twittery, smoky, artistic, cool kats, photographic, dramatic, musical, anagrammed, globalized, or maxed.

Not forgetting the cast of characters involved in producing this; they all have virtual lives of their own.

And of course, to you, dear reader, for at least 'giving it a go'.

Author's Note

This is part of a collection of crime thrillers featuring the characters of Jake, Clare, Bigsy, Christina Nott, Chuck Manners, and Amanda Miller.

Titles include, The Triangle, The Square, The Circle, Raven, Raven's Card, Archangel and Play On, Christina Nott.

They started in London, then I moved to the west country, so I set recent novels around Exeter, giving them a slightly cosy crime feel in deep Agatha Christie country. The closest to an incident in a hotel is 'Cosy', set in Magister Grange.

The sequence is Cosy, Church and then Dark.

But don't expect "this one" to solve anything.

I hope you enjoy!

Ed

Ed Adams Novels

Triangle Trilogy		About	Link
T1	The Triangle	Dirty money? Here's how to clean it. Money laundering	https://amzn.to/3c6zRMu
T2	The Square	Weapons of Mass Destruction – don't let them get on your nerves. A viral nerve agent being shipped by terrorists and WMDs	https://amzn.to/3sEiKYx
T3	The Circle	The desert is no place to get lost. In the Arizona deserts, with the Navajo; about missiles stolen from storage.	https://amzn.to/3qLavYZ
T4	Cosy	Cosy Crime in Devon	https://amzn.to/3wQVNED
T5	Church	Devon crime expands	...
T6	Dark	Escape, or is it?	...
Archangel Collection			
A1	Archangel	Sometimes I am necessary. Icelandic-born, Russian trained agent Christina Nott, learns her craft.	https://amzn.to/2Y9nB5K
A2	Raven	An eye that sees all between darkness and light. Big business gone bad and being a freemason won't absolve you.	https://amzn.to/2MiGVe6
A3	Card Game	The power of Tarot whilst throwing oil on a troubled market	https://amzn.to/2Y8HLgs
A5	Play On, Christina Nott	Money, Mayhem, Manipulation. Christina Nott, on Tour for the FSB	https://amzn.to/2MbkuHI
A6	Corrupt	Parliamentary corruption. Trouble at the House	https://amzn.to/2M0HnOw
A7	Sleaze	Autos, Politics, Gstaad	https://amzn.to/3sE3UDt
Big Science			
B1	Coin	Get rich quick with Cybercash – just don't tell GCHQ	https://amzn.to/3o82wmS
B2	An Unstable System	Creating the right kind of mind	https://amzn.to/2PRJciF

B3	The Watcher	We don't need no personal saviours here. From the Big Bang to the almighty Whimper	https://amzn.to/3kTFWjg
B4	Jump	Some kind of future.	https://amzn.to/3sCzK3h
B5	Pulse	Sci-Fi dystopian blood management with nano-bots. Want more? Just stay away from the edge	https://amzn.to/3qQlBvL
B6	Rage	A madman's war	https://amzn.to/3MEuKlL

Blade's Edge Trilogy

E1	Edge	World end climate collapse and sham discovered during magnetite mining from Jupiter's moon Ganymede.	https://amzn.to/2KDmYOW
E2	Edge Blue	Endgame, for Earth – unless?	https://amzn.to/2Kyq9au
E3	Edge Red	Museum Earth an artificially intelligent outcome – unless?	https://amzn.to/2KzJwjz

Master Collections

C1/T4	The Ox Stunner	The Triangle Trilogy – thick enough to stun an ox Triangle, Circle, Square in one heavy book. all feature Jake, Bigsy, Clare, Chuck Manners	https://amzn.to/3sHxlgh
C2/A4	Magazine Clip	First three Archangel novels	https://amzn.to/3pbBJYn
C3/A8	Ignoble	Corrupt and Sleaze omnibus – double album	https://amzn.to/3sp6EUL
C4/B7	The Dealer	Jump, Pulse and Rage Collection	https://amzn.to/3AlZmWg
C5/E4	Edge of Forever	Edge Trilogy	https://amzn.to/3c57Ghj

Rule 9b: Enjoy yourself, it's lighter than you think.

Dark

PART ONE

Devon

No bird soars too high
if they soar with their own wings.

William Blake

Leon Kacper Rząca

It was a moment of emotional clarity as I realised the vicar was truly badass. I was back near Exeter after being asked to return by MI5's Amanda Miller. It's complicated, but I will explain everything in a minute. I'm Jake Lambers, and there I was, parked in a car park with the vicar, Leonard Richards, who was married to Penelope Richards - a local vineyard owner..

I had met the Richards before when Emmanuelle Catteau and Jago Fox invited me to a party at their house, but in truth, Penelope, and Leonard both looked different from what I remembered. Strange, because I used to be a journalist and part of my tradecraft meant I could usually remember people's names and faces.

Now I'm sitting alone with the vicar. We wait to go into a meeting in a local hall. The car park overlooks a small local shop and there were a couple of lads on tricked out bicycles hanging around. I make a joke to Leonard; something about it being an ideal spot for drug trafficking.

"I used to have a parish in the Midlands," Leonard says, "in Walsall; that's close to Wolverhampton, if you can't quite place it."

I could. When I worked for Street, the Lads' magazine, we used to do articles about footballers with fast cars. It was in the days when Top Gear was still a thing, before they all turned into bloated, seedy, skiddy Scalextric drivers.

I'd been meeting a fast-car owning Walsall player who was a relative of the great 1930s player Gilbert Alsop, a prolific goal-scorer for Walsall.

"Go Saddlers!" I say, expecting a reaction from Leonard. But there was none. He continues with his description.

"We had a church hall in a Walsall suburb. It was on a piece of land which was probably once a bomb-site after the second world war. Anyway, we had a makeshift car park there, which was very convenient for our hall. The trouble was, it got used for dealing and was raided by the police - it was in the days when they had time for such things. We were a charity of course, and we put into the council to get the perimeter secured. In those days they had the money and we were fortunate to get robust metal fencing put all around the car park, like the kind you see outside Post Office van depots."

I nod, remembering a local sorting office with that kind of grey, pointy palisade fencing.

"Well, it then became a local spot for more amorous activities. Our caretaker illicitly took admission charges for evening parking as well as parking near to the town in the day. None of the money made it back to our charity. Turns out he was employed by the drug dealers too. We'd inadvertently built a secure trading post for the whole of Wolverhampton."

"What did you do?" I ask.

"I let nature take its course," he explains. There was an existing drug ring in Wolverhampton. They were annoyed at the antics in Walsall. They bought a few testers from our car park and then one night arrived in force. Our man was roughed up, but then the police, including an armed response arrived. The police had one of their American style SWAT vans that's normally at Birmingham Airport."

"A quick scoot along the M6?" I ask.

He continues, "They found a Skorp and several phones in the ringleader's BMW. They could see on the phone he'd been trying to get bullets for several guns including a German Luger pistol, a Glock, and a '44 spinner'."

The way Leonard was describing these armaments, on top of the steel fenced drug yard, made me wonder just how much he knew about what had been going on.

"A skorp - that's a Skorpion sub machine gun?" I ask.

"Yes, The Škorpion is a Czechoslovak machine pistol. Compact, fold-back handle. You'd have seen it in the movies. Ferocious fire rate."

He seems to know as much about guns as an armourer. Time for an obvious question.

"How is it you - a vicar - know so much?"

"I was in the militia before I joined the church," he explains. He rolls up his left sleeve. I can see a kind of anchor shape made up of two letters - a P and a W.

It's "Polska Walczy," he explains, "Poland Fights."

I look confused.

"It's an emblem from the second world war. When the Germans invaded. My family name is Rząca, which can sound like Richards when badly pronounced. My first name is Leon, but I went for Leonard so that I won't get confused. It's been tradition to pass it on. My original name was Leon Kacper Rząca - but you should call me Leonard!"

I just knew that the wires would be buzzing back in GCHQ once they got this information about our vicar.

Alone in the truck

"Look," says Leonard, "I think I should go ahead. I can explain to the ladies why you are here, about the Press Release, that kind of thing. Then you can come along in about ten minutes. You've met Penelope? My wife...She'll be in the meeting too. Look, I'll leave the keys - you can lock the car for me?"

He climbed out of the battered-looking Land Rover. A vicar driving a Land-Rover, hardly Miss Marple's territory, it should more likely be an ancient, polished brown and beige Rover 3500.

I take a breath and look around at the still life of the parking lot: the two lads have cycled away, there's a few darkening shrubs swaying in the wind, an arrhythmic tinking of the cooling engine, Leonard even left the keys swinging in the ignition.

I feel a certain placeless intensity that drifts in

like a fog. It's subtle at first, lingering somewhere between fidgety expectation and accidental meditation. I've just discovered the vicar has a past. And what a past; there must be more. How has he married the sensuous Penelope, for starters? And she has land. Not a little but a whole acreage of vineyards.

I'm sensing that I'm in a movie pushing into a close-up but can't figure out what it is I'm supposed to be taking from it. Details that usually strike as banal now seem utterly alien. Like the grape vines reaching out to touch. How delicate and fleeting it all seems, a kind of melancholic trance sweeping over me. But it's with a rush of clarity, as if I've shaken out of a dream. You are here. You are alive. You are in it.

I'm thinking back to the series of events that brought me here, my choices, mistakes, and achievements, such as they are. All the twists and turns. And yet now I'm supposed to be joining the ladies in their meeting with the vicar. Not at his church, nor at the hall, but in a local community centre near to where they live.

A few steps back

I should take a few steps back. Explain how we got here.

Right now, our main group has decamped to Exeter. In the same area as we were when we visited Jago Fox and Emmanuelle Catteau for their engagement party.

We are staying in Dittlesham, a quaint village-sized town whose history goes back to a two-thousand-year-old Roman settlement. The Romans visited Dittlesham to provide a secondary supply route to the garrison at Isca Dumnoniorum (Exeter). They landed goods along the river, built a small fort, and constructed a straight road into Exeter that is still used today. Despite modern transport, ironically, the speeds on the route have not changed, as many traffic lights slow down the journey while new housing developments are being built.

How do I know this? I've been here before when we were investigating the strange goings-on at Magister Grange.

And why would such a small place be a town? In 1300, King Edward gave a grant I to the Earl of Devon (Hugh de Courtenay) to hold an annual fair and a weekly market, and this Royal Charter elevated the two towns of Topsham and Dittlesham from villages to town status.

Then, from nearby Topsham Quay, ships set off to fight the Spanish Armada, settle the Americas, trade with the continent or fish for cod off Newfoundland. Smaller boats ferried goods and passengers up, down and across the river, netted salmon and fished for mackerel. From the high churchyard wall, you can see up and down the estuary and imagine how life on the river has changed over the years.

Along the shore, shipbuilders sawed and hammered and while wooden ships ruled, these shipyards were some of the busiest in the country.

Forges made anchors and chains, rope-makers twisted hemp, a factory produced specialised nails. During the 18th and 19th centuries, they built cargo ships for merchants and warships for the Navy here. Houses still have names like Nail Store and rooms with names like Sail Loft.

In adjoining fields, market gardening was big

business, and after the railway arrived in the mid-1800s, daily goods trucks laden with fruit and vegetables chuffed their way to Covent Garden. In this working-class environment, there were once many pubs and a reputation for rowdiness. Local students regarded a pint in each of the 'Dittlesham Dozen' as a rite of passage.

It is all a far cry from our normal base in London where we have offices in Hays Galleria, on the South Bank, just a quick hop over the Thames to the City.

There's four of us in the main outfit, that's me, Clare Crafts, Dave (Bigsy) Carter and Christina Nott. We started out with three of us (Clare, Bigsy and me) and came into rather a lot of money from our first adventure. Some might say it was a misadventure, I'd call it providence.

Clare knew Christina, a musician, who also has a rather intense back-story, and she became a fourth member of our poorly named 'Triangle'.

Then, over the course of a few years, the British Secret Intelligence Service, also known as SIS or MI6, assigned us a few intelligence operations as untraceable 'stringers'. And MI5, come to think of it.

'Stringers' is really slang for contractors, although the entomology goes way back to the 1950s meaning 'newspaper correspondent paid by length of copy' probably from the earlier figurative sense of 'one who strings words together' - a dismissive or contemptuous term for a writer. I guess I'm a stringer in more than one sense.

But why us? Well, to start with, we were unknowns, but we also had particular skills. Me as a journalist, Clare with her graphics and acting skills, Bigsy is a real techno-nerd and Christina has a background as an agent of other States and with major military skills. I'll tell more of this later.

So once Amanda Miller found us, she realised she was on to a good thing, able to deploy us in various situations which needed absolute deniability. And we reaped the rewards tax-free.

We'd just returned from a zinger of a party in Devon when we got the call from Amanda to go visit her in Vauxhall Cross. The headquarters of MI6 has a 'side gate' that all the taxi drivers know about. A bit like 'the steps' at Waterloo. Of course, it's the flagship office and there are many other buildings squirrelled around London and Cheltenham, which is the base of GCHQ (Government Communications Headquarters).

The euphemisms of Charles House, Slough House, Nova South, Palmer Street, Regent's Park, Number 85, Bude, are legion, even in spy novels. Sometimes the buildings are 'closed' to ease suspicion, but a few trips down some deep lift shafts will soon show that they are very much alive and kicking. Just don't get out of the elevator on the wrong floor.

The Intelligence and Security Committee of Parliament (ISC) thoughtfully publishes a list of the agencies, which helps everyone map out the relationships between the Security Service (MI5), the Secret Intelligence Service (MI6) and the Government Communications Headquarters (GCHQ) and beyond into Joint Intelligence Organisation and the National Security Secretariat in the Cabinet Office; Defence Intelligence in the Ministry of Defence; and the Office for Security and Counter-Terrorism in the Home Office.

Phew, that is a mouthful of bureaucratic civil guardians, and yet still they hire us as outside stringers.

In our meeting, Amanda briefs us, both on the outcome from the last situation, but also for another fresh assignment in - wait for it - Devon. We have a few extra people present. Jago and Emmanuel from our adventure at Magister Grange, Chuck Manners our hard-as-nails ex-marine associate from the USA and Grace Fielding from GCHQ. Grace has fired up a projector.

"I cannot thank you enough," says Amanda,

"This was above and beyond. Chuck told me about your respective parts in this. Well played, all of you."

"We think we worked it out," says Clare, "You extended the invitation to us so that you had some eyes on what was happening."

There follows an extensive debrief on our last successful operation and one who got away - Alina Petrovna. She had neutralised her onetime ally, the ruthless Colonel General Omurazat 'Strelli' Kovarin.

Amanda surprised us with her unexpected link to what we've been asked to do.

"The Devon and Cornwall police continued to think the main investigation was connected with drug dealing, " says Amanda, "It is how we will lead off this time. But Alina Petrovna is clawing her way into ever more powerful positions in the 'Moscow Mafia'."

"The bratva," clarifies Christina. "The brotherhood - Greedy Kovarin was running a deal which needed huge amounts of money, which he was borrowing from the obschak - 'Moscow Mafia' fund. Then he used elite troops during the negotiation. Only Putin can get away with those kinds of moves.

"When the Kremlin and the gangsters from Moscow Solntsevskaya mafia discovered that

Kovarin is using their resources on a stupid deal, they cut up rough. That's when Alina Petrovna was asked to take control - effectively usurping the now damaged goods of Kovarin."

"I've never seen a taser used across a boardroom table before," said Christina, "It certainly quietened things down."

"Yes, with Petrovna taking Kovarin down, it meant all the other pieces of the jigsaw would fall into place. Even the Chinese backed away when everything became so violent."

Then there's some noise, and a dark-suited woman enters the room.

"A Russian package to the Triangle Offices was intercepted," she says.

We open it. It is flight tickets. Open diplomatic returns to Istanbul. From Alina Petrovna.

Dangerous tickets

"I don't think we'll be using those," says Clare, "Remember Jamal Khashoggi?"

We all remembered the horrific incident when agents of the Saudi government killed a Saudi dissident journalist at the Saudi consulate in Istanbul, Turkey. Khashoggi was ambushed and strangled by a 15-member squad of Saudi operatives. The consulate had been secretly bugged by the Turkish government and Khashoggi's appalling final moments were captured in audio recordings, transcripts of which were subsequently made public.

After repeatedly shifting its account of what happened to Khashoggi in the days following the killing, the Saudi government admitted a premeditated murder, but denied that the killing took place on the orders of Mohammed bin Salman - the crown prince of Saudi Arabia.

However, the US Central Intelligence Agency

concluded that bin Salman had ordered the murder. In the same month, the United States levelled sanctions against 17 Saudis over the murder but did not sanction bin Salman himself.

"Alina is making a point," says Amanda, "and by flagging the tickets as Diplomatic, it just makes you easier to find."

"I can't see what this has to do with us needing to revisit Devon?" I ask.

"It's Brant related. They are up to something, but we don't know what. Our single lead is a vicar named Leonard Richards."

I vaguely remembered that I'd met him, and his wife, during Jago and Emmanuelle's party.

Jago is nodding, "Sorry mate, but I won't be able to join you on this quest. I need to make myself scarce for a while. Canada beckons. But The Reverend Leonard Richards was punching above his weight when he married Penelope."

I try to think back to the Reverend. One of my ways I remember people is the 'looks a bit like' trick. For Leonard Richards, I'm seeing in my mind someone who 'looks a bit like' Harry Potter's Minister of Magic Cornelius Fudge. A scruffily suited, short-haired, blond man who wears gabardine raincoats and continuously looks both dishevelled and perplexed. He originally appears to be harmless, if ineffective.

Then he becomes dangerous as he desperately clings to his office.

Then Grace Fielding puts up a picture of Leonard Richards. Forget everything I just said - my mind must be playing tricks. He is more like Alan Rickman playing Severus Snape in Harry Potter movies or playing the leader of the gang in Die Hard. Powerful, long-haired, stylish, and carrying a deep sense of foreboding.

Jago gasps too," Are you certain that's him?" he asks, "Only he looks as if he's had a significant makeover!"

"I found these on Instagram," answers Grace. She flicks up a couple of wedding photos. They look like a perfect couple: Leonard and Penelope like a dark Selene from Underworld and equally dark Snape from Potter.

"Hot!" mutters Bigsy.

"Very hot!" echoes Grace.

Not not not

I should describe my friends gathered at this meeting. There's Clare, who is someone I've known for years who still has a private and mysterious inner life.

She's smarter than me. Well, not smarter exactly, but certainly more intuitive, and it's a real joy to know her. I've learnt her secrets, the colour of her humour, even the precise vibration of her mind-gears.

Then sometimes I'll look across a room and glimpse her just being herself - doing something mundane or chatting away at a dinner party or telling me about her day and even though I may have seen her do it thousands of times, I still see her in a different light, struck by her sheer uniqueness.

But no, we are not lovers.

Nobody else knows her in the same way as me.

There's only one of her in the universe. And here she is. It's easy to forget that she doesn't just exist in the contexts I see her in, but as one ingredient in a broader social soup, steeped in her own unique vibe wherever she goes. Around her are a menagerie of relationships with hundreds of people I'll never meet. Whatever she is to me, to them she might be a wildly different figure: an intimidating woman, a childhood buddy, the comic relief, or the one who got away.

And when she's alone, she's like Peter Sarstedt's Marie-Clare character alone in her bed. I can imagine her looking over her reflection in the bathroom mirror, making goofy faces, or reminding herself to live in the moment, to be herself, to get through the day. While falling asleep at night, she might be thinking over the parts of herself that make her feel proud, or self-conscious, or ashamed, trying to be a better person. She might be going back through her memories, sifting through fragments and echoes, curating an entire alternate history that she keeps locked away: remnants of another life.

But no, we are not lovers.

Every word she speaks is thrumming with emotional resonances I can't hear, informed by a context she'll never be able to explain. She has desires too raw to defend, fears she can't bear to think about. And all of this is happening all the time, invisible, right there in front of me.

But no, we are not lovers.

I'll never fully know her, not really. As long as she lives, she'll never find the right words to truly convey what goes on inside her head. But if it's any consolation, she'll never know me either. There will always be this fundamental separation between us. Two separate people, with different lives, different bodies, a different past, and a different future. Each of us is a wholeness unto itself, with a tiny but unmistakable gap.

And yet, by some miracle, we transcend that separation. Over years spent together, I feel something in the air between us. It's like putting two images together and flickering them back and forth until they appear to spring into motion, infused with a life that wasn't there in either alone.

But no, we are not lovers.

Yet there will always be an uncertain distance between us. Maybe the cynics are right, and love is only ever an illusion. But maybe it's the sacred kind of illusion with power, if only because of our self-belief. And that's enough. All that is required is that we keep showing up, and never stop asking each other, "What are you thinking about?"

It's not about getting an answer to the question.

It's the act of asking, of trying to reach across the gap, working through the mystery—that is what's worth holding on to. We must keep that feeling alive, even if we never find the right words to express it.

Then there's Christina. She's got so many passports that it's almost implausible. She comes from the land of the ice and snow - literally from Iceland. Then to Russia - to Arkhangelsk, where she received special Russian Akademy espionage training - and a Russian passport. They sent her to Bulgaria for training on NATO weapons and machinery. And another passport. And then a series of missions in Europe (French passport) and the USA (American passport). And that is before she became a musician (British passport) travelling the world using the music as cover for her other activities.

Christina is also unique. She has that vibrant colour of personality. It shines vividly in everything she does, from the shoes she wears, to the lunch she brings to the office, to the precise wording of a text wishing me a happy birthday. You'd think it would all seem generic, but somehow every detail is quintessentially Christina.

She will always insist I'm anything but neutral, painting me with the same broad brush I use to paint her: you're a sunny yellow, she might say, or a chill blue, a fiery red, an innocent pink, an edgy black. She is not wrong; and there is a certain quality threaded through our personalities, and we often play into it, because it's a lot easier to be cheerful or crabby or crazy or boring if everyone already thinks that way.

I know I can't compete with the roles Christina inhabits. If she tried to shadow me through an entire week, she would be astonished to see me as a serious professional, a sexual being, a spiritual person, a story-time twit, a nervous wreck, or the life of the party. Each of these impressions may be accurate in the moment, but each reflects only a narrow band of my full spectrum, chasing Christina's warp-speed Doppler shift.

Christina let her identities change when she joined The Triangle but has kept her ethos, skills, and her ultimate fitness. Case in point, one day we were joking around and she said she could jump over my head. Without a pause she ran towards me, scissor kicked herself upside down, used my shoulders as a lever to fly over my head, landing lightly behind me.

Christina had just enough pause in the middle of the manoeuvre to plant a tender kiss on my cheek. Upside down, of course.

She has also saved our skins a few times. Her habit of carrying firepower has proved useful on several occasions. That and her piloting skills.

Then Bigsy. Our ultimate techno-nerd. He knows everything about computers, transmitters, and similar equipment. He can fix anything from a combine harvester to an Apple Mac Studio. And he is good at blending in. You need someone to look inconspicuous, then he's our man.

Bigsy has our culture encoded in his heartbeat. His images make up the raw material of wild dreams, deep fears, even attempts to rebel. So, it's hard not to get swept up in the spectacle of it all, absorbing stories and values and symbols until we no longer question their importance. It's as if there's a circus whirling around all the time, so overwhelming that we keep forgetting it's there.

This is true for all of us swept into the Triangle but Bigsy tunes out the fanfare and takes time in nature, in solitude, or in some other culture entirely—getting away long enough so that when he returns to normal life again, he'll look around with fresh eyes, and see how abnormal it really is.

Bigsy can take in all the scenes and sideshows. He knows it doesn't quite feel like reality anymore, more like the world-building of a fantasy novel. Their tireless dedication to fleshing out even the most mundane details impresses me, although I don't know who came up with this stuff. That's where Bigsy excels. He edits the vaunted marble halls of politics and business and religion and the arts, each buttressed by its own rules and standards and practices, booming with the echoes of a billion conversations that everyone seems to take so seriously. The power of a billion butterfly sneezes. He can decode the rituals of status and fashion, the mythology of the markets, pop-culture think pieces, and waves of breaking news. I sometimes wonder how he got so invested, following these stock characters, and their little dramas and debates. Who said what to whom? What does it all mean? What will happen next?

Bigsy knows how arbitrary and provisional it can all feel. Though it has all the weight of reality, he knows it could just as easily have been something else. He helps me to realise that ordinary human beings designed and built all of our big ideas and sacred institutions. So much of our culture exists because someone was hungry once, someone was bored, someone was afraid, someone wanted to impress a mate, prove someone wrong, or leave their kids a better life.

Bigsy decodes this whole circus. It is so big and bright and loud, it's easy to believe that it is the real world and we live somewhere else outside of it. But beneath all these constructed ideals, there is a darker heart of normalcy, a humble humanity, that powers the whole thing. He knows we are all just people. We go to work and play our roles as best we can, underpinned with his gadgetry, spinning our tales, and performing our tricks, but then we take off the technology and guises and go home, where we carry on with our real lives.

Inevitably, within a few days or weeks at most, Bigsy will see us getting swept right back into the big show, even though we all know it's all just an act.

And Me? I'm just a journalist who got fired.

Devonian

Those plane tickets from Alina made us all pause. We could see that she was sending us a few messages. 'We know where you are. We know who you are. We can get to you.'

Grace brushes this aside, "Our lead is the vicar. He's been cropping up in intel reports. Nothing to do with drugs, although that could be your cover reason to the police."

I think back to the party at Jago's place. Magister Grange, where we had been through a complete murder investigation, yet still linked with events at Brant Industrie.
"I know a couple of people who could help us," I say, "There's Bettina Kübler, a Swiss researcher, at Brant, Geneva, working on eDefense. And Stéphane Gérard, a very close friend of Bettina, who works in weather systems using game theory to manage climates. She works for Brant right here in Exeter."
They had both been at Jago and Emmanuelle's

party and Stéphane Gérard had hinted to me that there was something unusual about the Richards and their charities.
"What's the actual investigation about?" asks Clare.

"We don't know precisely," answers Amanda hurriedly, "but your assignment will be as if you are investigating 'do good' charities."

"It's cosy. The vicar has started a successful rehabilitation charity in Devon," answers Grace, projecting a PowerPoint slide. "Think of it like a migrant processing centre. They take in migrants, get them presentable to the British authorities, and then let them find their own ways."

"I see, similar to the Danish system?" I ask, " Or maybe it was Sweden?"

"Exactly, Leonard Richards claims to have modelled it on the Swedish work," answers Grace.

She pulls up another slide, then continues, "The Swedish Red Cross runs centres for refugees and other migrants who have suffered trauma linked to torture, armed conflict or dangerous migration journeys. Our vicar even originally named his centre 'Skövde Clyst Richards' after the Skövde centre in Sweden."

After that name, I'm thinking of IKEA.

Grace continues, "In this Skövde centre, professional teams of psychologists, psychotherapists, physiotherapists, social workers, medical doctors and interpreters work closely with those affected to help them to heal."

She adds, "Because Penelope Richards had all of that land, - you know - where the vineyards run down to the River Exe - they were able to get permission for quite a large facility, in the grounds of what was once an old Spitfire squadron. They dropped the 'Skövde' from the name after a few weeks because local people thought it sounded German. Not ideal on a still runway ex-Spitfire base, just along from a marine commando base. They designed a facility similar to the hotel that Exeter Rugby Club built in their grounds - except its significantly bigger. Most of the people are only in the centre for weeks and then many of them can integrate into the community."

Now I'm thinking of trafficking.

"It's a pretty big deal then," asks Clare, "And Reverend Richards must be a major 'do-gooder' in the community?"

"That's what we want to find out," says Amanda, "As well as to understand how it all gets paid for."

"Yes, this must be big money," chips in

Christina, "Especially judging by some of those internal pictures that Grace just showed us."

Corrected: "That's what we wondered too," says Grace, "And that's before we even consider the Reverend's church."

"It's laundering," says Christina, "They taught us this in Arkhangelsk."

All eyes turn to Christina.

"There's about 170,000 registered charities in England and Wales, along with the millions worldwide. We were taught by the Akademy that these are easy to exploit. They often have low levels of security to all the funds they hold and little awareness of good money laundering and financial crime prevention controls."

Christina continues, "It's even easier if you control the charity as well as the funds. It's like using a casino to clear funds, but with even better returns. When casinos, soccer, even car businesses came under scrutiny, the place no-one looked was charities. Too much ragged paperwork.

"It's the same principle though: criminals convert proceeds of crime into assets that seem to have a legitimate origin, so that they can permanently retain them or reuse them for additional criminal activities using the three main stages of Placement, Layering, and

Integration." That loud, yellow-haired, chubby American pseudo-politician knows most of this playbook."

Christina looks around, "But surely you also know most of this?" she asks. Grace and Amanda nod, the rest of us remain silent.

"So, take Reverend Richards," Christina continues, "In a charity sector context, a really simple example could be a large donation to a charity of 'dirty money' or proceeds of crime which is then layered in with legitimate funds that the charity holds.
"The fraudsters set up a fake beneficiary as a front to receive the freshly laundered funds from the charity, making them appear clean and legitimate. If the charity is a sham, the fraudsters brazenly pocket the donations or move it to another clean source.
"A major building project provides amazing cover for layering the money and the design of the buildings can be re-purposed easily enough. Another fancy hotel in a booming area.

Grace nods, I can see she agrees with Christina, "Reverend Richards projects a 'do-gooder' image which places him above suspicion.
Whether it's the church or the migrant centre, they can both be seen as forces for good, although both appear to have implausibly large turnovers."
So that's what we'll be investigating, but we can't tell the Reverend.

Krasimira's comeback

Grace continues, "I've been profiling the migrants that Clyst Richards processes. It's very atypical. In most zones where there are migrants, there is an edge of difficulty. There is also an unpredictable arrival rate. Take Sicily, where the facility for 250 ended up with 2,500 migrants. Ten times overloaded. The same in Lampedusa - that island of southern Italy, where 6000 migrants were channelled into a facility for 600. Ten times too many"

"It's been the problem with sub-Saharan Africans for a while now," adds Amanda, "And it places extreme burdens on all the infrastructure. Food, in particular."

"Yes, but not in this centre in Devon. It's entirely balanced with a steady throughput of 'processed' migrants integrating into the local workforce."

"It's not what it seems," says Christina, "They are

using it as a clearinghouse for people they want to install in the UK. Clever really, they can wash money and people out of sight of the State."

Grace continues, "I profiled some of the recent migrants in Clyst Richards. They are from Ukraine, Slovakia, Poland, and Romania. They have been bussed to Italy and then swap to Swiss transport, which merges them for a flight from Geneva to Exeter. They are frequently repositioned as low-end workers. Domestic help, cleaners, bar-staff, those kinds of roles. Nothing seedy, by the way."

"But Poland? I thought it was taking in Ukrainians?" asks Bigsy.

"Yes, around 1.5 million refugees, but some of them are moved on and sometimes Clyst Richards has picked them up. It's been the same with Slovakia, taking in Afghans and Syrians as well as Ukrainians. They have over 100,000 now"

"And Romania?"

"Same again. They have about 100,000 refugees," answered Grace.

"So, whatever our vicar is doing is a mere rounding error in the numbers?" asks Bigsy.

"Correct. He is worthy but suspicious," says Grace.

"I can see where this is leading," says Christina, looking knowingly between Amanda and Grace.

"We thought you could be a Bulgarian," answers Amanda, " It fits the profile of the migrant camp, but means you'll be unknown."

"Ha, they used to call me a *Kifla,* at the Bulgarian Academy," explains Christina, "When I was assigned to the Bulgarian Academy most of the others were also Bulgarian, although there were a few other nationalities mixed in. The true Bulgarians made some fun of us, saying that we were pretend-Bulgarians. They seemed to know about the Russians placing people in their Academy. They had a nickname for us - *Kifla* - which meant 'loaves' but was their slang for selfie models. It implied that we were there to get selfies of ourselves standing by Bulgarian scenes."

"Oh, I thought it was a 'girls and guns' fetish kind of thing?" answers Grace.

"Grace is right, but we were above all that lethal lipstick. We even decided it was best not to have a return slang for the Bulgarians, because it would only escalate. Andrei Raikov and Aneta Yanev were my accomplices during this time. We were all Russian, but when we chatted, we discovered that we'd all been somewhere else before the Russian Federation. Andrei had been in Finland and Aneta had been in Sweden.

Chuck smiles at this, says, "You still seem to know people everywhere. This could explain a thing or two."

Christina continues, "Now this Bulgarian Academy was much more about Boys and their Toys than the Arkhangelsk Akademy. My impression of Bulgaria was of an old-fashioned version of Russia. They spoke a quaint Slavic, and there were many remnants of the Communist era left in the streets. But they knew how to set up a modern military academy!"

She looks around, sees everyone is still looking at her and then continues, "We had everything, firearms, rifles, anti-tank, anti-aircraft, actual tanks. Both Russian and American. I was told that Bulgaria had skilfully played the NATO game and given hardware by just about every country. No wonder it was such a good place to train. There were fields to play war games and laughably, if the weather was bad, there were also indoor shooting ranges."

"I think I learned just about every type of weapon and also got a reputation as an excellent shot and gun handler, which I reckon was because of my prior time on the farm."

"We decided," said Grace," To give you back your old name."

"Krasimira Radka?" says Christina, "I know her so well!"

"Yes," says Grace," You'll be a Bulgarian national who had spent her whole life in Russia. You lived on a small farm in Russia, before you went to Bulgaria."

"Yay," says Christina, "You've been peeking at my files, Grace!"

"But how do we get Christina into the Clyst Richards facility?" asks Bigsy, ever practical.

"We'll put her onto one of their regular bus runs," says Grace, "From Exeter airport to Clyst Richards. I can get a set of documents made that will look as if she has been on the entire journey from Geneva. Complete with a Bulgarian passport, although I expect you still have one, Christina?"

"Maybe and maybe not. Extra passports are always useful," smiles Christina enigmatically.

So that's how we first got involved with the Richards. Placing Christina inside a migrant facility in Clyst Richards. But not having a clue what we would find there.

Disguise

Before machines the only form of entertainment people really had was relationships.

Douglas Coupland

Primani

We are in Bigsy's Mercedes. The one he drove back brand new from the Stuttgart-Sindelfingen factory after we finished our original project when we founded The Triangle. I'm with Bigsy, Clare and Christina and we are around the outside of Exeter airport at an American-styled hotel.

Christina looks at me.

So much can be conveyed in a glance. We can feel such ambiguous intensity, looking someone in the eye - it's somehow both intrusive and vulnerable. Their pupils glitter black, bottomless, and opaque.

The eye is a keyhole through which the world pours in, and a world spills out. For seconds, you can peek through into a vault that contains everything they are.

Christina has dressed herself in Primark clothing - Primani - as she calls it. It looks fine, just like any of her regular clothes, only with a hint of deliberate mismatch. A white top. Beige wide dad trousers like we'd see on one of the celebrities stuck on desert island trash television. A light brown belted longline cardigan, with a collar that could make a hood. And faux leather chunky black boots. "Channelling Nina Dobrev", she says.

"The Vampire Diaries?" I ask, "But she's Canadian?"

"No. She's Bulgarian, born in Sofia as Nina Kamenova Dobreva. Keep up," says Christina, smiling.

I can see our exchange has lightened the moment. Her eyes fleetingly flash her vulnerability, her pain, before switching to her humour, vitality, her power over others, and what she demands of herself.

But whether the eyes are the windows of the soul or the doors of perception, it doesn't really matter. I'm still standing outside of the house.

Eye contact isn't really contact at all. It's only ever a near-miss that you feel as it slips past you. There's so much that we keep in the back room; so much that other people never get to see. We only ever offer a sample of who we are, of what we think people want us to be. And yet, how rarely do we stop to look inside, let our eyes adjust, and try to see what's really there, the worlds hidden away in the eyes of others.

We are peering out from behind our own special doors. You put yourself out there, trying to decide how much of the world to let in. It's all too easy for others to size you up and carry on their way. They can see you more clearly than you ever could. Yours is the only vault you can't see into, that you can't size up in an instant.

You'll always have to wonder if someone peers into your soul. Or if anyone will put in the effort, trying to find the key. We're all exchanging glances, trying to tell each other who we are. Trying to catch a glimpse of ourselves, feeling around in the darkness. Christina's little girl-doll seen in my eye.

Pupil: *From Latin pūpilla ("little girl")*

And yet, I absorb Christina's steel as she readies for the mission. We each say a brief goodbye to Christina. I feel her core strength returned through her hug. Dusk and a light rain as Bigsy drives slowly back to the short stay, where a motor coach is picking up the next batch of migrants.

This time, Christina's glance gives nothing away as she unhurriedly boards.

Clyst Richards

It's a strange, empty feeling as Christina departs. Maybe we were always destined to be sitting right where we are right now. Or maybe it's a miracle that we managed to get together at all, knowing how many obstacles might have gotten in the way.

Or maybe it's nothing personal, and it was all just a coincidence. You never know.

We never know how easily fate might have tipped us onto some other course, meeting some stranger, who might have felt like a soulmate. As we sit here in Bigsy's limousine of a car, each wrapped up in our own concerns, we have no way of knowing how our varied path have crossed.

Or whether this risky next gameplay will be successful.

Clare reads from her phone, "Here I've found an

entry...

"Clyst Richards has become a leading actor in the psychological treatment of migrants in the United Kingdom. Patients come to the centres voluntarily. Once a person arrives seeking care, they are assessed to determine whether they are eligible for support. When accepted, they take rehabilitation services based on their needs. The duration of the treatment varies from weeks to a few months, depending on the individual situation of the person concerned and their needs. All services are provided free of charge."

"Leading actor?" laughs Bigsy, "This is prime public relations work!"

Clare continues,"...Clyst Richards has adopted a holistic approach with groups providing a safe space to talk about the present, past and future. The support group activities aim to help understand that they are not alone; that others share their thoughts, feelings and worries, and even if their stories are not identical, they are welcome to share their feelings."

"Touchy-feely, " chuckles Bigsy.

"Persons benefitting from our services usually respond positively to the support we offer. 'The body needs food to survive, but the soul needs other people. We offer both here'."

"Fair dos," mutters Bigsy, "That last bit sounds

okay,"

Clare continues to read, "Migration officers, teachers, doctors, civil servants, police officers, and other people who might work directly with migrants need to be made more aware of the indicators for trauma. Often, they do not feel they have the right tools to deal with adults or children affected by trauma and are unsure of where they can refer them."

"It begs the question," says Bigsy, "How on earth do they afford it all?"

I wonder this too and think back to Christina's crash course to us all on money laundering. What was it? Placement, Layering and Integration.

Conspiracy

I'm back at the hotel now. It is by the side of the rugby pitch. The hotel is so big it could have its own gravitational effect. I wonder how it ever got planning permission. But then again, I know. It will be a well-documented power-play.

We all went our separate ways tonight. Christina's decision to go on this mission alone has dampened our spirits as we all worry about what she might find or if she will be detected in the Clyst Richards campus.

It's comforting to imagine that conspiracies run our world. To think there is some hidden order to things, a superstructure held high over our heads by a shadowy cabal of insiders. Of course, there's no hidden order; but then again, of course there is.

It's all of us. We are all insiders, managing an intricate web of relationships, deploying hundreds of unseen gestures and soft power plays, soaking up gossip with the urgency of counterintelligence. It's at once mundane, and yet no less chilling than any other conspiracy, because it leaves us questioning the very fabric of reality, wondering what we don't know.

Ask how many cover-ups have you taken part in? How many times have you heard something you weren't supposed to hear, withheld certain details to make your case, deftly changed the subject, or tried to steer someone's behaviour without them knowing?

If you can do all that without a second thought, everyone around you must be doing it, too. Of course, you'd like to think you've got a clear view of the broader social landscape, but it's possible you don't have a clue.

There are so many backstories that people keep to themselves, so many back channels you don't even know exist. Random clusters of friends might be carrying on parallel conversations in another group text or meeting up regularly at events you're not invited to. People know far more about us than we think, holding on to secrets and rumours they use to inform our character but never mentioned in our presence.

It's enough to make you crazy, never knowing if you're living in an alternate reality being constructed around you.

But perhaps there's some comfort in that human

uncertainty.

Common Prayer

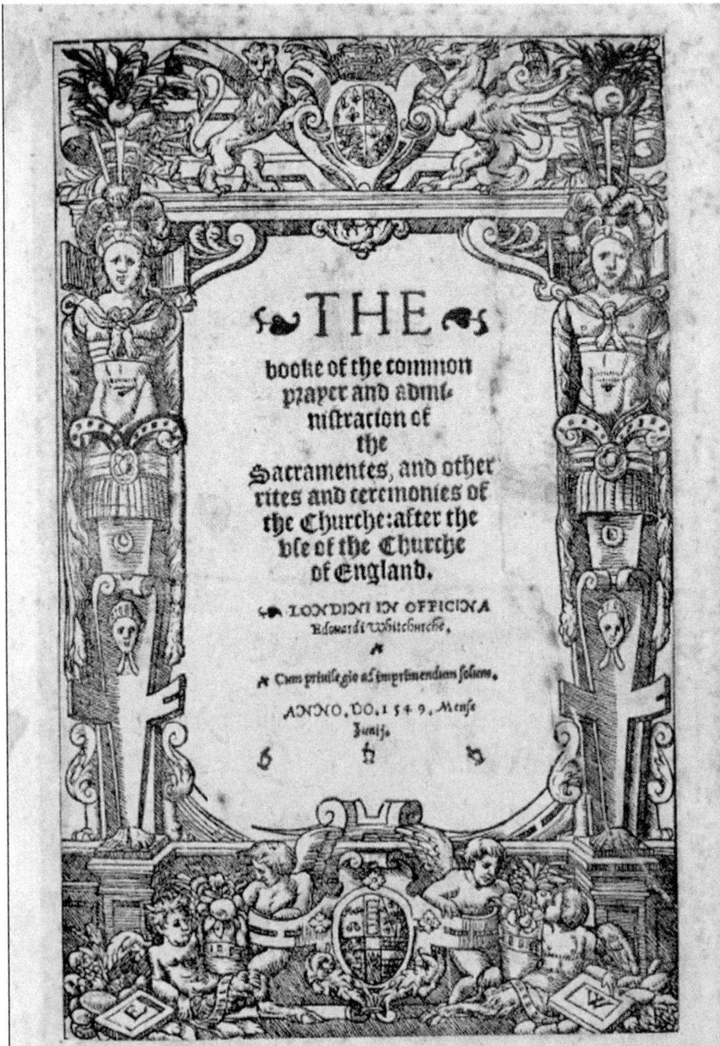

THE

booke of the common prayer and admi-
nistracion of
the
Sacramentes, and other
rites and ceremonies of
the Churche: after the
vse of the Churche
of England.

LONDINI IN OFFICINA
Edouardi Whitchurche,

Cum priuilegio ad imprimendum solum.

ANNO. DO. 1549. Mense
Junij.

A visit to the Church

Now it is a waiting game, for two entire weeks until Christina will emerge from the Clyst Richards campus. We all noticed when Christina moved out - noticing just how empty a place can feel. She can still contact us, via cellphone, but we suggested she is discreet. Christina knows how to play that game.

It surprised me. I take Christina for granted as a friend. So do we all. In her absence, we visit Reverend Richards' Church to attend one of his sermons. To listen to how he comes across and to put to him the idea of a public relations piece in the Sentinel.

I had no idea we would be visiting an eastern orthodox church. It's not clear to me if this is a special day until I hear the words in the lesson. It is the second Sunday after Pentecost - a special kind of All Saints Day. The Reverend explains that in olden times, monk Dositheus Toporkov said Russia had holy men and women worthy of veneration. These individuals did not receive attention and were not written about.

Reverend Richards explains how Archbishop Macarius of Novgorod collected Orthodox Russia's saintly heritage. He and his assistants worked through the mid-1500s on the Great Menaion Reader, a twelve-volume work detailing the lives of many Russian saints not recognised by the church. The volumes, compiled on a calendar basis with biographies of many Russian ascetics, accelerated venerating many Russian Orthodox saints.

I look around at the hymn boards. I realise they are in Russian and English. And now here we are: Bigsy, Clare and me, feeling a kind of joyful relief in all its blessings and mysteries and chances and changes.

We can see that the Reverend appears unthreatening. That our embedded Christina, with her concealed weapon in her deliberately fake Mulberry bag, won't have been in danger. We look around with a new sense of gratitude, taking in the complexity of things: raindrops skittering down the church window, tall trees leaning in the wind, clouds of cream swirling in our post-sermon coffee. Everything falls quiet, and all seems to mix, until you can't tell the difference between the ordinary and the epic.

The Reverend walks across to us. He can see we are new. "Yes, the church was the first thing here on Penelope's grounds. It's one of the oldest churches around Exeter. Its nearest twin is St Martins in Central Exeter, close to the Cathedral. Bishop Leofric, the bishop who founded the cathedral in Exeter, consecrated the first church on this site in 1065."

"They were blood thirsty times," observed Bigsy.

The Reverend continues, "Its tiny parish served the workers and traders who crowded into the cramped houses around what used to be a bustling seaport before the Prayer Book Rebellion. Following the enforced Prayer Book's changes to eradicate Catholicism, the parishioners compelled their priest to revert to the old service. The rebels argued that the new English liturgy was like a Christmas game."

We look surprised.

"This claim relates to the book's provision for men and women to file into the quire on different sides to receive the sacrament, which seemed to remind the Devon men of country dancing. A kind of 'strip the willow.' Justices arrived at the next service to enforce the change. An altercation at the service led to a proponent of the change being run through with a pitchfork on the steps of the church house."

We all wince at this bloody news. Bigsy was right, bloodthirsty times indeed.

The Reverend smiles when he sees our reaction, then continues, "Most of the parishioners marched to Exeter to protest at introducing the new prayer book. Although some inhabitants in Exeter sent a message of support to the rebels, the city refused to open its gates. The gates were to stay closed because of the siege for over a month but sadly in that time, the king's men razed this whole isolated village, except for the church, which stood as a reminder of the power from London."

We look at the roughcast exterior of red volcanic stone with bright, white Beer stone windows, which makes it look like a fancy gingerbread house. Inside, it is simple and full of light.

"For a place of prayer, peace and quiet reflection, it's difficult to believe that these Exeter churches actually possess a dark and violent past - a place where a rebellious vicar came to meet a gruesome end. Like St Thomas Church in central Exeter, this one was also the scene of executions.

The Reverend adds, "Originally from Cornwall, Roger Barrett became the vicar of our church in 1535. He was an unconventional vicar, skilled with a crossbow, and also known as a wrestler. Indeed, he wrestled Robert Welsh, who was the vicar of St Thomas Church. Robert won, although these two men of the cloth had very similar paths. Robert Welsh saved Exeter from being burnt to the ground by Catholic rebels, but later came to be executed brutally for treason. Roger Barrett suffered the same way, although there are no surviving records, just word passed from mouth to mouth.

"We must look back to 1549, when Edward VI was King, crowned at the age of just nine years, after the death of his father, Henry VIII. Edward was England's first monarch to be raised as a Protestant and this was to trigger the rebellion and unrest that would bring about Welsh and Barrett's downfall.

"In 1549, they were both a part of the Western Rebellion joining Catholic rebels who refused to accept the Protestantism being forced upon them by the King's men.

He looks and can see we are still interested, "Churches had to comply with orders and radical changes. These included the removal or destruction of Catholic symbols, priests being allowed to marry, and introducing the controversial Book of Common Prayer, written in English rather than Latin.

The authorities ordered priests to wear plain robes, banned the Latin Mass, and locked Catholic bishops in the Tower of London.
The people of Devon and Cornwall met with fury this when there was already a great sense of unease after introducing a tax on sheep and disputes over land.

Rebels drew up a list demanding the changes be reversed and other conditions, using the forceful term "we will have."

Many rebellions, including the famous one at Sampford Courtenay, took place, and the rebels set up an armed camp in Clyst St Mary - close to here.

I can see Clare and Bigsy nodding, we are all fascinated by the story.

In Exeter, Leonard Richards explains that 6,000 armed rebels, including seasoned mercenaries from Germany and Italy, arrived.

In the words of sixteenth-century Exeter historian John Hooker, Robert Welsh held the position of arch captain and played a vital role in directing the rebellion.

Hooker attributes the act of preventing rebels from burning Exeter to the ground to Welsh.

"But why would he do that?" asks Bigsy.

"The whole situation was a mess. In the end, the Government sent Lord Russell to put an end to the rebels' acts, and they were defeated. Rebel leaders were severely punished, including Welsh, who was also implicated in the murder of Russell's messenger."

Leonard grimaces, "Welsh was sentenced to

death, his execution carried out by Bernard Duffield, a protestant councillor who wanted to make an example of him. Duffield raised the gallows high on the steeple of St Thomas Church and Welsh was bound in chains and strung up for all to see."

He pulls a small black book from his jacket, "It's my sermon notes...John Hooker wrote: 'He was hung in chains, having on his priest's vestments, with a holy bucket, a sprinkling brush, a small bell, a pair of beads, and other Romish articles hung about him, where he remained for a long time. The long time was three years.' "

The church has painted on it the arms of Dittlesham. The Reverend smiled. The first one I'd ever seen from him.

Then he adds, "Penelope had the church as an old folly on her property until we refurbished it. You can see we have added something to it, as well as recreated the path to the old boathouse down on the River Exe. Walk with me, I'll show you!"

We follow him along a well-made path to a new sleek boathouse. Not at all what I was expecting and there's an even bigger surprise inside. A sleek silver-grey super yacht, with enough room for 11 passengers.

Bigsy whistles, "That's incredible!" he says, "I didn't know these were real - just something in

James Bond movies!"

Reverend Leonard smiles, "We've been lucky. As well as our work here, we have a further charity in Cherbourg. This powerboat makes it so much easier to get there rather than using the airport."

We look at one another. I can tell we are all thinking the same thing. I notice the ship is named ETAP and then I realise it's written in Cyrillic and remember it means 'Star'.

There's a little picture of a goose flying over a red star. Star of Казарка is the full boat inscription. Then I notice there's a rack of jet-skis. They all say Казарка, with that same motif. I have a feeling of overload.

Christina knew she would be going into an unknown environment, fact gathering for us. Indomitable spirit, attuned to the nuances of this unexpected life in a strange campus.

And we, poised to hear what she has discovered, have to find a time to review it with her. We know the wish of Leonard Richards and his wife Penelope to publicise the work at Clyst Richards. And that's how I came to visit the church to ask the Reverend if we can meet some of his clients, and then to write about it for the Sentinel.

Bordeaux wine

We leave the Church, get back to Bigsy's Mercedes and make our way to the hotel, each lost in our individual thoughts.

"Bar?" suggests Bigsy, and we all agree. Clare, Bigsy and I arrange ourselves in a corner of the restaurant and each order a tall drink. Bigsy and I are experimenting with the local red cider.

"That was interesting," Bigsy says. "The grounds, the church, the boathouse, the accommodation blocks for the campus."

"Not to mention that airstrip. It is all so well-funded," observes Clare, "well beyond any local charity funding."

"The boat alone would cost millions," says Bigsy, "it's a top of the range high performance luxury sea-going vessel. They call it a yacht, but it doesn't have any sails!"

"So, what can we infer?" asks Clare, "Shadow funding, charity as a smokescreen, church as a front,"

Bigsy adds, "Convenient spot away from scrutiny, access to water which easily leads to France. Helipad. Heck - even that old Spitfire runway still looked well-tended. They are up to something big."

"And they must have great backing," I observe, "Maybe laundering? trafficking? Who would suspect a church in the middle of Devon?"

"Amanda was definitely interested, so it must be big," says Clare, "But she didn't seem to know what was happening."

"We'll know more tomorrow, when we get to meet Christina," says Bigsy, "it's been two weeks now. She has great self-discipline to remain silent."

I say, "I'm interested in how Reverend Richards seems to have changed. He was like a Non-Player Character before, but now he's turned into a mainline suspect."

Clare nods, "Yes, I noticed that too. Both he and Penelope have received a serious makeover since we saw them at the Magister Grange party."

"Penelope is the rich landowner who has made

this possible," says Bigsy.

"Did someone buy her out?" I ask, "Remember she had dual nationality, part French? Maybe the real Penelope went back to France and we are seeing a substitute?"

Clare and Bigsy look at me, and I can tell I've just said something stupid.

"Not so stupid though," says Clare, "I can remember Penelope Richards saying her original name was Calvet. We were chatting when all the disturbances were going on at that party.
"I inquired whether she had any connection to the Calvet wine, considering she was a winegrower herself. She smiled and told me there was a distant link. I looked her up after that. She was indeed a relative and some of her wealth comes from her original wine links."

Bigsy is checking his phone, "Yes Calvet: Sumptuous, with a rich fruitiness, this is silky textured with fragrant notes of new vanilla oak. It's made in a modern style but with definite Bordeaux character... That's what Waitrose say about it!"

I'm thinking that Penelope has all of those characteristics...

"And it's a Bordeaux wine so we could check the area for Calvet? " asks Clare, "see if she has returned home?"

"I see. We check whether Penelope Calvet is now living in Bordeaux?" I ask.

"Exactly," answers Bigsy, "That they have somehow engineered a swap and 'Penelope' and 'Leonard' are substitutes."

"They can't pull off something like that without others noticing?" I ask.

"But we were prepared to take it at face value," answers Bigsy. "I guess they must have paid their staff well to keep quiet?"

"Either that, or this cider is stronger than we think!"

Facts

You have people come into your life
shockingly and surprisingly.

You have losses that you never thought you'd
experience.

You have rejection and you have to learn how
to deal with that and how to get up the next
day and go on with it.

Taylor Swift

Christina's first report

We've agreed to meet Christina outside of the Clyst Richards campus. She is permitted to catch a bus back to Dittlesham every Thursday, although also expected to only be away for a maximum of four hours.

We wait in Dittlesham and she appears, looking slightly down-at-heel. I don't think I've ever seen Christina looking like this before. She sees us all and smiles. We are in a fancy afternoon tea kind of place, in a glass atrium area. I've been here before when we met Christopher Law here. He was a Magister Grange occupant, when he was in hiding.

Strange that now we have another kind of hidden person here, admittedly trying to converse in plain sight. Clare and Christina hug and we all settle down to an afternoon of Devon cream tea.

"How long have you got?" asks Clare.

"I need to be back by 6pm" answers Christina. I see her scoping the room, checking that there is no-one there who could recognise her.

"We'll take you back by car," says Bigsy, " That should give you a little longer."

Christina smiles: I can see she is putting a brave face on her experience.

"How are they treating you?" I ask.

"Oh. Well, thank you, good food and good company. As a matter of fact, it reminds me of Russian Akademy life, but without the weapons."

I can see that Christina isn't as low as I at first thought.

"It's been quite a pleasant experience for a couple of weeks. Think of it like a wellness retreat, but with hilarious lessons about the British. For me it is all very straightforward, but I shan't be sad to leave."

She explains to us the process at the campus. They take in migrants and provide re-education so that they can become very acceptable to the British workforce.

"There are various categories too. We have some people who can be client facing - they may work in hospitality - you know as bar staff and servers. Then there's some who are more 'back office' - who will work behind the scenes having some kind of office skill or similar. The last category are the manual workers, who go off to get work on farms or in factories, sometimes on building sites."

"But nothing -um - inappropriate?" asks Clare. We all stare at Christina.

"No, I couldn't find anything linked back to trafficking or similar negative things. Just the speed at which they are converted. Days instead of months."

"So, what are they trying to make you?' asks Bigsy, with a sparkle in his eye.

"I'm one of the client-facing ones; they worked out I have good English and that I could lift the ambiance in a wine bar!" Christina smiles.

"So, is that what you've been doing, then?" asks Clare.

"Kinda," says Christina, "Although I've also been befriending some of the others. It's been very interesting. I'd expected we'd all be bunked together in some kind of communal facilities, but in practice we all have our own rooms. The expense!" She looks wistful.

"They are grouping us together in small teams. For me, they are planning to send me to a particular London bar, where I'll work and share a London apartment with two others."

"But that doesn't make sense," says Clare, "The cost?."

"That's where it all goes a little weird," answers Christina. "And it's for a reason. They want us to help them find things. In return for a lifestyle above our wildest aspirations, they want us to find out about some key targets."

My eyes widen, they seem to use these inmates as 'plants' to gather intelligence.

"It's like in the Akademy, we used to be told about honey traps," explains Christina, "But in this case there's no 'honeybun', instead we must listen to what they discuss."

"So, intelligence gathering?" asks Clare.

"Yes," answers Christina, "And some of it is pretty basic. Those other people who work in the lesser roles also have intel gathering priorities. But in their case, it is through collecting the trash and sifting through it to look for confidential material. It's laughably unsophisticated."

We are seeing a picture form. People imported to the UK. Made presentable and then sent into the labour market. Their added purpose, to gather intelligence.

"But what about Brexit?" asked Bigsy. We were thinking it too.

"Don't you see?" asks Christina, "The migrants are all 'Brexit ready Europeans.' Mainly from Romania, but also Estonians, Croatians, Bulgarians, Slovenians, Czechians."

"Why the split?" I ask.

"The dynamics of migration changed after Brexit, as you know," answers Christina, "India became the most common country of origin for migrants in the UK after many Polish left. But Poland is still the top country of citizenship of foreign citizens in the UK."

"Think about it," says Bigsy, "Adult migrants, over 26 years old, making up the bulk of those incoming, and more than half of them women."

"Are you sure about that?" asks Clare., "I mean, how can you know that?"

"I read it somewhere dependable, like the Daily Mail," answers Bigsy, grinning, "It's the same place that I read that the number of migrants is holding steady at about 14%."

"Well," says Christina, "the numbers we see on the campus don't bear that out.
"Well," says Christina, "we see more women on campus, and they are mainly from Romania. I

think the majority of them will be destined for manual work, judging from the people I've met."

"Is it all - ahem - legal?" I ask.

"Completely," answers Christina, "The reason they come to the campus is to become as British as possible. Then they are off to one or other fields of employment. But there's a twist."

"I think I can guess it!" says Clare, "They get two paymasters?"

"I've taught you well," smiles Christina, "Yes, technically they are being paid by their new employers, whilst getting a substantial top-up to gather information."

"How does it work?" I ask.

"Cleaners," answers Christina, "Access to offices, to secrets."

"Or bar staff?" asks Clare, "they make good listeners."

"Exactly," says Christina. "They asked me to go to a bar called 'The St George' in Nine Elms," says Christina.

Christina produces a small cube. She explains, "Its battery powered, lasts about 30 hours and will record when people are speaking."

Bigsy looks at the device, "Oh yeah, I've seen these before. They make one even smaller now, with replaceable memory cards."

"They gave me a dozen to drop around any interesting conversations in the bar. It's quite easy actually," says Christina.

"So, you'll be by the side of the SIS building in Vauxhall?" I ask.

"Yes, listening to all the spy talk!" grins Christina," Although I'm sure Amanda would be on to it!"

"What about the cleaners?" I ask.

"They are to go to a couple of suppliers to the Met Office in Exeter," says Christina, "It's not altogether clear why, although I asked one of them what they have been asked to do."

"Similar to you?" I ask.

"Not really," says Christina, "It's literally rummaging through the rubbish. Although one of them had a brighter idea." She smiles aware she has created some intrigue.

"They have a separate contract to dispose of the confidential waste, you know, in those bright yellow bins."

"Yes, it's much easier to get the targeted organisations to filter their own high security items, deposit them and then we can collect them," explains Christina. "A weekly collection, take the secure paper away and then process it." She grins.

"So, it's spy school for economic migrants," says Clare, " Bring them in, train them, re-paper them, then embed them where they can gather intelligence."

"Exactly," says Christina, " Mainly industrial espionage and almost impossible to detect. And most of it seems to have Brant as the other paymaster."

I ask her about the boat inscription we had seen. 'Star Kasapka'?

"That would be in Russian. Star of Казарка," Christina explains, "It means star of Brant - or Brant Star, more precisely."

I remember the logo. A bird flying over a star.

"It's the Russian red star, with a common migratory Russian bird - the Brant goose - flying over it. Brant's logo - at least it is in Russia.

Now I have symbolism overload as well.

The whole enchilada

We were all aware of Brant's potential part in this situation. We had a previous run-in with Brant when a whole furore blew up surrounding Jago Fox and Emmanuelle Catteau at Magister Grange.

A server appears with a well-stacked three-tier cream tea arrangement. We all look at one another and laugh.

Bigsy delicately helps himself to a slim sandwich from the lowest tier of the plates. Then he speaks, "In the olden days, soldiers would follow the routes taken by merchants around the world. Then conglomerates like Raven Corporation and Brant Industries came along and changed the thinking. These merchants could operate as 'soup to nuts' providers, supporting military initiatives, supplying and building weapons, operating armies, destroying targets (often covertly) and then assisting with reparations and so-called peacekeeping."

"Soup to nuts?" asks Clare, "Is that like nose to tail?"

"It is in gastro-pub talk," said Bigsy., "You know: 'the whole enchilada'!"

He carefully helps himself to a ham and mustard sandwich, which has been cut into a long finger shape. We all grin and then Bigsy continues, "A few well-known companies could see how this was a sure-fire way to make money, and to be quietly feared as lobbyists. Brant is one of them. Critical global networks can be constructed including communication, computing, logistics, financial systems, and even civilian transportation systems. Look - we even know that Brant attempted the forcible lobbying of MPs a couple of times previously."

Christina adds, "No one could really understand the extent of these systems, nor of the hold that it had on the geo-political environment.

We were briefed on that back at Arkhangelsk. Nowadays, it is a race between global conglomerates, controlled by the United States, Russia, and China, with emerging contenders from India, each which quietly builds critical data centre hubs from which they patrol and monitor around the world. Brant has become a player and has many of the lobbying

characteristics needed for success.
It resembles a Sinaloan drug cartel, shifting its influence but with perhaps less overt violence.

"Whoa," says Clare, " I think the narco connection needs some scrutiny!"

"Think about it," says Christina, "The number of people we've run into loosely connected with Raven and Brant and yet destined for short lives. Brant plays it hard."

Bigsy is onto the second layer now. Cakes and fancy pastries. "Brant realised Europe is second tier to the superpowers and heavily reliant upon American-influenced NATO. Somewhat like the 'Airstrip One' predictions of George Orwell. Of course, America's control of these global networks wasn't scrutinised much after the collapse of the Soviet Empire in 1991."

Christina continues, "Yes, they could build their own infrastructure, unchallenged. In fact, countries including most of Europe joined global systems for the internet, finance, and supply chains. That monetarist Milton Friedman popularised globalisation as the way ahead."

Bigsy continues whilst concentrating on a scone, "Then, after the Twin Towers, America started using these global networks to fight terrorism. They recorded vast numbers of phone calls. American control of SWIFT financial payments and dollar clearing were used to coerce other powers. Threats forced foreign banks to comply with US demands even if they technically weren't required to do so — being blacklisted from the US system was too disastrous to resist. "

"Exactly," says Christina, "It's the same as the Akademy playbook, except the Akademy is more overtly mobster."

Bigsy smiles, "Maybe fewer differences than you think. With the US Treasury as a player in security and intelligence affairs, their officials flew around the world bypassing diplomats in order to deliver their messages: 'Do what we say, or else.' Is that mobster enough?"

He helps himself to another cream and jam laden scone and continues, "The Snowden leaks provoked global discussion of America's power over critical networks. China started building its own rival networks with companies like Huawei. America neglected its Five Eyes surveillance while the global market for some technologies had shrunk to a few players, including the Chinese.".

Christina chips in, "Still Europe was ambivalent. Brant could see the gap in the market and an opportunity to expand coverage. Europe had been so hopeless on technology and defence, and so reluctant to face its failures, that it is now extremely dependent and resentful."

"Yes," says Bigsy, "On one hand it claims the moral high ground over 'respect for privacy,' on the other it quietly acquiesces with institutions handing shed loads of data to US intelligence that can be analysed and given to EU governments while they maintain their public pretence. "

He continues, "Europe loudly pledges to build capabilities to reduce dependence, yet they can't build and ironically become more dependent. Contritely using regulatory tactics when they can't keep up.

Bigsy concludes, "Brant knows these dynamics show a fundamental problem for the EU and UK. Control is slipping away, and Brant knows a power vacuum when it sees one."

Brant Imperium

"It's about how Brant wants control," says Christina, "They operate like a stealthy superpower. Underground and overground,"

"Wombling free," chips in Bigsy.

Christina grins, "And aerial," she adds, "The skies too. There are satellites and even railgun beam weapons like the Trigax. Now they are even talking about a fiery bracelet to circle the earth."

"Charming," says Bigsy.

"I see what you did there," I say but Clare kicks me under the table.

Christina continues, "And the United States, in particular, likes to boast about it. All those buildings around Washington. It's like a new format Rome with Palladian facades constructed how Julius Caesar's architect

Vitruvius would approve.

Bigsy adds, "Then, just like London, there's an underground network- not of trains, but of secret tunnels. Like mushrooms with mycelium spreading the information around and fostering an empire. Of course, the London tunnels and links are minor compared with America's."

"Not really," answers Christina, "In Britain, there's the high-capacity link to GCHQ and then the connections overseas along patrolled routes right into the heart of the American empire."

She pauses and then continues, "In Russia, it's still all a lot more analogue. Putin has to exert his mobster rule the old ways, with death threats as a punishment and unexplained money flows to keep the wheels turning. The west has privatised the connections, and that's where Brant sees the opportunity. The Kremlin are still busy turning state machinery private so that the oligarchs profit from it. They are at least an economic cycle further behind what America is doing and Brant is profiting from."

"But there's the irony," says Bigsy, "We think Brant is partly Kremlin owned; remember all the links we have already found?"

"True," says Christina, "Making the Russian weakness into a strength."

"So, you think that our good Reverend Richards

linked with Brant's underworld?" asks Clare.

You noticed the signage?" asks Clare.

Bigsy answers, "Think about it. Brant's empire is made of everyday stuff; the trade routes, infrastructure supplies, networks and comms that pack together in a densely connected web of economic activity. And they get paid to smash things up and then paid again to repair them.

"Back when Imperial Rome built a network of roads, it allowed merchants to convey their wares, but the same roads allowed legions to march quickly across provinces. When a traveller entered the empire from the backroads, they departed a world of villages and winding cattle tracks for one of trading cities, joined by long, straight thoroughfares that carried both commerce and coercion."

Christina nods, "In modern times, much of the proper business of empire has moved underground. American power still uses military might to maintain surface trade routes, deploys the U.S. Navy to patrol global sea lanes like the Red Sea and protects significant installations. American empire power also travels along buried fibre-optic cables, insinuating itself into networks across the world."

"But Leonard and Penelope?" I ask, "How are

they linked in and why?"

"That, my darling Jake, is something you will have to discover," answers Christina, "Unless I do first...Remember from next week I'll be based in London working in a wine bar. After a week or so, I'll ask Amanda to extract me."

Meanwhile, we plan to meet a few of the Clyst Richards inmates at an event in a village hall.

The ladies speak

Now we're back where I started...

I'm getting out of Leonard Richard's Land Rover and walking across to the hall. They don't know about Christina, who is embedded in Leonard's facility and she won't be along this evening. It's just me to accompany Leonard. His wife, Penelope is already in the meeting room.

I enter the building and find my way to their noisy room. I'd guess about 20 people, the majority women and all in their late 20s to early 30s.

Penelope has laid on some refreshments. There's a selection of cakes and a choice of tea, coffee, wine, and some kind of alcohol-free wine beverage. Dandelion and Burdock, I shouldn't wonder.

Penelope has a small table and there's a microphone rigged on it, with a compact little

Public Address system. She sees me arrive, stands, and walks to greet me.

"Hello Jake, this is a good outcome. I explained to everyone that you are from the Sentinel and want to do a piece about the facility. I can give you a handout with the basic facts and figures, but this gives you a chance to ask some extra questions...Colour...I think that's what you call it?"

I realise Penelope is quite media savvy, just as she walks back to the microphone and calls the attendees to order.

"Hello everyone, I hope you'll give a big welcome to Jake Lambers from the Sentinel. I'm giving him one of our handbooks, and then I think he will want to ask you all some general questions about your time in Clyst Richards."

There is a ping and I realise the microphone has been muted. Penelope passes it to me, and I switch it on again. I explain I'll be pleased to meet them all in small groups or individually in the next few minutes. When I finish my speech, there is gentle applause.

Then I talk to them. My first group is four ladies, I ask them to write their names down because I'm worried about getting the spelling right. I'm also struck by how well they all speak. It's perfect English with hardly a trace of accent. Not what I was expecting. They explain that they are from a group who will be working in wine bars and hostelries from next week. It's the local area around Exeter, except for a couple who are to go to London.

I realise that the two bound for London must have Christina as a companion, but I can't ask direct questions about Christina.

Then, I move on to the next group. Another seven who are to work in back-office functions, principally around Exeter. They are in groups of twos and a three so they each have a 'buddy'. There are a couple of men in this group. They tell me how they reached the Italian pickup point ferried by plane from Geneva to the UK. These also have good English, but I can detect slightly more of an eastern European accent.

Finally, I meet the last group. They have more pronounced accents and tell me they have already got work as cleaners, in offices, a hotel and a bar. There are another two men in this group. They seem to have better English and explain that they are the supervisors for the rest of the group. They are arranging minicabs to take the cleaners to their sites and also a van service to pickup and destroy the confidential waste, back at a facility provided on Penelope's land.

I'm intrigued at how this funding model works. The expense of accommodation for the workers, the ferrying of them by taxicabs to their places of employment, doesn't seem economically viable. I ask them instead if they are happy with the work conditions.

One, named Tsvetelina Danailova Karapetrova (Vetty) explains, "It's a perfect role for me. I come to Britain, work in a very exciting city, among people I know and receive a weekly paycheck which is at least double that which I'd get in Sofia. On top of that, I don't have to pay for accommodation and I get a separate allowance towards food. - It's unbeatable - I pay UK taxes and get part of my pay sent back to a local bank in Sofia."

Two or three of the others nodded their agreement as she explained this. I wondered how something could be too good to be true.

"They have asked all of us to behave well. To not bring the campus into disrepute, Of course we will behave. We don't want to mess it up for ourselves or any of the others. Reverend Richards is like a Saint."

I see Penelope smile. I sense she has heard this all before. She asks me, "Do you think you've heard enough Mr Lambers? If so, I'll ask Leonard to drive you back. You are staying close to the airport, I think?"

She touches Leonard Richards gently on the arm and whispers something to him. He smiles and then comes across to see me.

"So, you've got everything you need for the article? What else did you say you'd need. Ah yes, I remember, the Brochure and one of our Electronic Press Kits. Of course, we will do our best to accommodate you if you want some specific photographs or extra questions to be answered. Otherwise, I think I can return you to your hotel now,"

"That would be excellent, " I answer, still mystified at how this all adds up.

More than a kitchen maid

On the way back, I ask Leonard if we'd met at the party which Jago and Emmanuelle threw a month or more ago.

"I don't think so," he says, "I was abroad at the time, Penelope attended by herself. It was a strange affair, by all accounts."

Now I'm even more confused. I'm sure there was someone saying they were Leonard Richards at that party. And Jago seemed to remember him too, based on what he'd said when we all met in Vauxhall Cross.

Then I remember someone else from the party. Zoe Demelza. The bright Exeter student who had been working part time as a kitchenmaid at Jago's house party. I consider how I can contact her via the Exeter university website. Clare and I together should soon track her down.

Leonard asks me, "I think we have been quite

open with you, shown you the Church and also the work we are doing at Clyst Richards. I imagine that the people you have just met will have left you with a positive impression of our work, and also that you can see we are getting the results quickly."

"Yes, it's amazing that after just a few weeks these people are turned into the local economy, or even, it sounds like, some of them are finding work in London."

"That's right, and most of them have such a good grasp of British ways that they fit right in."

I decide to steer away from the money side of things. Instead, I ask, "Do you stay in touch with many of them, after they go on their way?"

"Oh yes, many of them want to repay some of the good. That could be financial or sometimes in other ways. There's no doubt that most people show great gratitude for our work. As a matter of fact, it's something I learned from the Swedish. When they started the Skövde centre, they showed me that people can be very grateful for their compassionate treatment. The Swedish system is linked to their government and has been going many years longer. I hope your article will show us in a positive light. I know we are handling a mere handful of cases, but hopefully the effects will multiply."

Everything Leonard was saying made sense and

yet I was still deeply suspicious of his motives, but like Amanda, I didn't know why.

Big screen

The next day we have a call with Amanda. Bigsy has rigged it so that we can run the conference call from the big TV in his room at the hotel.

"It's secure," he insists, "We are simply using the telly as a big screen instead of having to watch this on our smart phones."

I can see Amanda is sitting with Grace Fielding. I was half expecting Chuck Manners to be there as well, but he is nowhere to be seen.

"No Chuck?" I ask.

"He's in Geneva right now," says Amanda, "Meeting someone from Brant."

"Enough said," I reply. He is obviously fact gathering for Amanda.

"What have you all found out?" asks Amanda.

Clare says, "Leonard Richards seems to have been replaced, and the same goes for Penelope Richards.

We suspect they are currently living in Bordeaux, and Penelope might be using the name Calvet."

Grace nods, "Yes, we have found her. Renée Calvet. Renée means 'born again' by the way. Renée seems to have a 20-room bolt hole in Bordeaux, as well as another very sunny place in the rather exclusive Juan-les-Pins, near to Antibes. All gated compounds around there. The Saudis have a Royal enclosure near to her place, actually."

Bigsy mutters, "The 'bolthole doesn't sound particularly modest either, if it has 20 rooms?"

"Exactly, but it's used as a retreat for a number of prominent and somewhat anonymous business people."

"That's why we have a trip planned for you," says Amanda, 'You'll hear why in a minute."

"Where?" I ask, thinking Scarborough or Leeds.

"It'll be sunny," promises Grace, "Put it this way. There's a hierarchy of locations. We've just scratched the surface. Exeter, Cherbourg, Antibes. But get to Antibes and then use a fast powerboat and in around three hours you can be across in Bastia, Corsica. And it's almost undetectable."

"But why?" asks Bigsy.

"Well, if you had some illegitimate business to transact, an interesting location for such work is Bastia." answers Grace, "It may be pretty, but it is also pretty deadly. Corsica, the most beautiful island in the Mediterranean, also boasted Europe's highest murder rate per capita. At least, until recently with the Ukraine and Middle East wars."

She adds, "And if we look at the wider business from Reverend Richards, we can see he has additional locations."

"This is becoming quite a network," says Clare.

Amanda speaks, "Hold that Corsica thought. And also, that much of the land for his business has been assembled following the unexplained deaths of family members of Reverend Richards."

Grace continues, "The truth lies because the 'unacceptable face' of Corsica exists while scarcely ever colliding with the tourist idyll. Corsica is a rare UNESCO natural beauty with towering and inaccessible mountains, drained by endless ravines flushed by ice-cold waters, tumbling down to turquoise seas, fringed by endless bays of golden sand."

"Yeah, I took a break there a couple of years ago, " answers Bigsy, "Its people are always welcoming, whether in a little roadside snack-bar perched atop a rugged col, or in an impromptu beach café. Dramatic castles and fortress towns hint at the island's complex history of conquest and colony amid a landscape all but devoid of evidence of any big-money endeavour to exploit any of the island's seemingly endless attributes. Gosh, I sound like a travel brochure."

He hesitates but then adds, "Whilst I was there, breakfasting in a saucisson-bedecked café I met a beautiful Parisienne, Valérie, who lived and worked on the island for many years. Unemotionally, she told me she saw both her hotel and her car torched, on different occasions, yet still finds herself drawn back. 'It's a very frightening place to work but it's a wonderful place to go on holiday,' she said. 'That's when I realised about the parallel universes that exist in Corsica'."

I'd never heard Bigsy talk about that before, nor heard him mention Valérie.

Grace carries on, "Vendetta. A particularly Sicilian word, but also used in Corsica. There's a roll call of invading colonists that date back to the Phoenicians – via Romans, Vandals, Byzantines, Saracens, Pisans, Genoans, Italians, Germans to name but some. It's produced a society characterised a disdain for subservience of any kind, corruption, and complicity in the structures of the state, the long-armed struggle for independence and, latterly, organised crime, often casually labelled 'the mafia.' "

"This is getting deep," says Bigsy. I'm thinking it too.

Grace continues, "Building development in Corsica seems to be controlled not so much by permits and legal frameworks as by whether shadowy figures will choose to blow up a new building once it's complete. My colleague in GCHQ worked there many years ago and told me how a German family was building a large home by the coast. Once the structure was complete, one day there was a huge bang and it all disappeared in a cloud of dust."

"Grace, you could do a great line in travelogues," says Bigsy. Even Amanda smiles.

Grace adds, "Corsica's single greatest asset is its variety. This is an island where families can ride toy trains, hikers work up a sweat and history buffs swot up on Napoleon.

"It's a fragrant playground that majors in superb shores — hundreds of them — before throwing in elegant hill towns, cycling, wonderful wines and natural wonders for good measure."

She pauses, "The thing about the building

development is interesting. Guess who the near neighbours of the Calvets are?"

Clare answers, "Not the Richards?"

"I always knew you were smart," says Grace, flirting with Clare across the Zoom link. Then she continues, "Part of France, but reasonably autonomous, the 'Ile de Beauté' also averages seven-and-a-half hours of sunshine per day, somewhere between 20C - 30C."

I'm thinking this could be a grand for a holiday.

Then Grace adds, "Corsica is far from a secret, but still carries that splash of adventure. Despite infrequent direct UK flights taking just over two hours, it's less familiar to British holidaymakers than mainland Italy or France, Sicily or even neighbouring Sardinia."

"Yes, we had to fly via Marseille," says Bigsy.

Grace continues, "The curious thing is that the Mediterranean's fourth-biggest island is the fault line between two universes. Crime and Vacation."

Amanda adds, "The legacy of the lengthy armed separatist struggle, preserved the island's pristine beauty. The Fronte di Liberazione Naziunale di a Corsica, or FLNC, only laid down its arms in 2014, after nearly four decades of bombings and murders, the deterrent effect of which surely meant Corsica did not develop in the same way as Mallorca, Ibiza or Rhodes."

"I've never been," says Clare, "But I have to those other places. Corsica is quietly under the radar."

"Hiding in plain sight," says Amanda, "From time to time, the French government will issue a statement to the effect that it's finally going to get to grips with violent crime by the island's criminal classes. This is usually in response to some particularly unpleasant assassination and, equally usually, ultimately proves to be no more than words."

Grace adds, "One such occasion was when the then prime minister announced a crackdown after the shooting in broad daylight of leading Corsican lawyer, François Deschanel – the 16th such assassination that year. He was gunned down with an automatic pistol by the pillion passenger on a motorcycle at a petrol station outside of Ajaccio. 10 bullets."

Grace adds, "I've the report it's here: the state prosecutor commented at the time in an interview with news channel France 24: 'There are many murders in Corsica. Too many.
But we understand that nearly these murders are directly related to organised crime, and people almost always settle accounts and disputes over territorial expansion.
It's very rare to have the cosy-crime 'husband-kills-wife' type of murder in Corsica, as is sadly

more common in other jurisdictions I've worked in, such as Marseille and Paris.'

Grace continues, "In the absence of a concerted central governmental response, it falls upon the islanders themselves to challenge the criminal status quo."

"Another brutal slaughter. This time of Massimu Susini – killed by a single bullet from a sniper rifle – prompted the formation of citizens' groups demanding his killers be brought to justice."

"That sounds hard-core organised crime, with a full-on assassin," says Bigsy.

"Oh yes, and money behind it," says Amanda, "The French state's seeming paralysis when it comes to tracking down and punishing killers in Corsica stems not just from this fear, but from a deep distrust of France, still seen as the colonial power after two centuries of 'occupation.'

"Against this backdrop, Marie-Louise Deschanel, daughter of the murdered lawyer, François Deschanel, says people like her father have 'died twice' – not only physically, but 'in legal terms' too, as they fade from memory with no judicial response. She questions how people can be murdered in full view of CCTV cameras and yet no prosecution be ever brought – she cannot be sure whether this is down to incompetence or complicity.

"Marie-Louise's willingness to speak out is in marked contrast to the silence that prevails and stifles comment on even quite mundane matters of public interest at all levels of society."

"But something else," adds Grace, "Those locations with 'Reverend Richards' buildings have one thing in common. They are funded by Brant Industrie. The only ones not connected are the 'boltholes' in Renée Calvet's name. In Bordeaux and Cap d'Antibes.

"It's an air gap," says Bigsy, "To keep things separate."

"You think so too," says Amanda.

Bigsy surmises, "Think about it. I can go visit the Calvets in Bordeaux, then slip away to Juan-les-Pins, and from there be across to Bastia, and soon be back in Reverend Richards territory, also known as Brant. And it's all high end enough that I can be a rich oligarch and not raise the slightest suspicion with my choice of venue."

"Shrewdly put," says Amanda, "Wait until you hear from Christina's first week in London, and then it will time to plan your visit to Corsica. Chuck will be back, too."

PART TWO

Corsica

Il faut toujours se réserver le droit de rire le lendemain de ses idées de la veille –

'You should always reserve the right to laugh the next day at ideas you had the day before.'

Life hack of Corsican-born Napoleon Bonaparte

Collecting our thoughts

Another week has passed. Christina has been in London, but decided to come back to Exeter on Sunday, to tell us what she has discovered.

I'm not convinced she will go back again..

We are still in the same hotel by the stadium, and Christina arrives in late morning, to our surprise accompanied by Chuck Manners. We all greet them both.

Christina explains, "Chuck called me up yesterday and offered to drive us both down here. We made pretty good time, but it's not as fast as the train,"

Chuck smiles, "No, the train seems to go at 125 mph. I can only do 70. But at least it was door-to-door."

We all smile. "And the same going back!" says Chuck.

I should explain that Chuck Manners is an ex-marine, who we met a long time ago, when we were in our first ever project. We all have a great fondness for Chuck, who can seem gruff to others but is a playful kitten around all of us. We didn't know it at the time, but since Chuck left the US military, he and Amanda Miller became 'an item'. Chuck moves in and out of our circle and was once saved by Christina, when, during an investigation, some gun men were sent to his hotel room in Brussels. Maybe Christina will work this situation longer, after all.

"Okay, you go first, Jake," Christina smiles, looking at me.

I tell her about the extra Calvet connections, the string of other buildings. I tell her about how Brant was involved in the situation.

"It's a very typical set of moves," says Christina. "Set up a complex web of companies, all handling cash and intangible products. Create an untraceable division between them (like in Juan-les-Pins), then use the operation as a clearing centre for money. A laundromat. It's even cleaner that the buildings scams favoured by certain American politicians. Those schemes are about buying empty real estate with off the books money. This way it's charity donations and offshore banks that are re-processing the money. Placement, Layering and Integration. Get the cash, layer it through charities and integrate it into the mainstream."

"But why is there such a volume?" asks Clare, "I mean, the scale of this operation is immense."

Christina speaks, "Understand that Reverend Richards isn't high in this food chain. He's a front. Like the shopkeeper who owns the technology store that is being used to pre-order goods before it declares itself bankrupt. Here, I think the main organisation is connected to Brant. We have found a way that oligarchs can clean their finances. Forget soccer clubs, casinos, and car leasing. Reverend Richards is the figurehead for a much broader scheme."

"Anyway, my two flatmates have told me some more. Desislava and Anelia - that's Desi and Anni - they are both working with me at the wine bar but know more of the other girls. In the evenings we've been sitting with a bottle of wine and chatting about life in Clyst Richards."

"What, not painting the town?" asks Bigsy.

"No, they are both in love with their men in Sofia. We are talking major separation anxiety here. We have separate rooms in our apartment but when the doors close, I think the phones come out."

"You're handling it?" asks Clare.

"Yes, remember I was at the Arkhangelsk Akademy and then in Bulgaria. I can handle most deprivations," says Christina.

"Let me tell you what they told me," Christina pours herself a glass of water.

"First of all, Leonard Richard's placements to find espionage secrets don't work. We get SIS types in the wine bar, but they seem to know less than me about what is happening."

"Then, I picked up from Desi and Anni that other Clyst Richards girls have been sent to Metrological Office suppliers around Exeter. They are supposed to be looking for anything to do with weather management. It's called Project Awesome."

"Awesome? Whose idea was that? I ask.

"No really, it's the Advanced Weather Systems Management (AWSM - Awesome) Project.

"The ladies have been asked to collect any useful discarded elements. There's also two of the men operating a confidential waste collection service."

"Who piece things together?" asks Bigsy.

Christina smiles, "It's laughable really. The cleaners have worked most of it out. They think it's some kind of 'gun in space' to create distant weather patterns. And by that, I mean over huge intercontinental distances."

"It's the Trigax," says Bigsy, "They are somehow repurposing the Trigax. Think about it, Trigax has three beams. Used together they could stir up the atmosphere. It's a very clever way to wage economic warfare,"

"This goes well beyond cloud seeding," says Clare, "You know the way they used to bomb clouds with iodine crystals."

"We experimented with that when I was working in the deserts around Los Alamos," says Chuck, "Strictly speaking we were on the edge of what was legal."

He smiles as he recollects, "We used cloud seeding to enhance precipitation. We used planes to spray small particles, such as silver iodide, onto clouds with the goal of creating rainfall. Around that time, the Chinese were using the same techniques to 'wash the air' clear of pollution- at least that's what they said they were doing."

Grace adds, "Way back in the 1950s, Project Cirrus was an early attempt by General Electric to modify the weather under the supervision of the United States Air Force. Attempts were made to create snowstorms and seed hurricanes by using silver iodide. While General Electric reported positive results, they also acknowledged that their experiments were controversial."

Chuck adds, "My close military buddy when I was on the desert base was named Sike. He was an expert on cloud busting. He was Navajo and also knew of their traditions of rain dances, with feathers and blue turquoise, symbolic of wind and rain. August was his special month for the rain dance. Sike was a smart cookie and bridged from Navajo traditions into the modern world. He even gave me some turquoise moccasins, which are used in the ceremony.

"Of course, what we were doing with aircraft and iodine all fell under close scrutiny. Weather modification was supposed to prevent damaging weather, such as hail or hurricanes; or to provoke damaging weather against an enemy, as a tactic of military or economic warfare. It was like Operation Popeye, when clouds were seeded to prolong the monsoons back when US was fighting in Vietnam. Weather modification in warfare was subsequently banned by the United Nations under the Environmental Modification Convention."

"So, what happened to Sike?" asks Grace.

Chuck answers, "We stayed in touch. He left the military and became a professor at Arizona University. They have a Native American/Indigenous Faculty. He's Diné - tradition says he's descended from 'The People' who arrived on earth in the story of creation. Age-old, they had some interesting beliefs. In the Diné language, there are six genders: Asdzáán (woman), Hastiin (male), Náhleeh (feminine-man), Dilbaa (masculine-woman), Nádleeh Asdzaa (lesbian), 'Nádleeh Hastii (gay man).

"Wow, Chuck, you really got this!" observes

Clare.

"From my respect for the people," says Chuck., "They used to call me," he looks bashful," Skookum. It means 'strong' and is from 'skookumchuck' strong man!"

Chuck smiles, we can see he is thinking back to those days.

"Another Navajo I knew, Tom, he and I were in the desert. Camp fire, the whole bit. We decided to invent an improvement to the Navajo classifications. we kept the first two and adapted them very slightly. It became Gender, Spirit, Senses. So, I'm a Man-Man-Man" said Chuck. Christina's a "Woman-Man-Woman. Get the idea?"

"Isn't it somewhat sexist?" asks Clare.

"Not really," answers Chuck, "And we are still riffing off the olden days. The Navajo were quite progressive about these things. I think you, Clare, would be Woman-Woman-Woman."

"I prefer Myers Briggs," she answers, You know: introversion/extraversion, sensing/intuition, thinking/feeling, judging/perceiving?"

"Oh yes," says Bigsy, "But you have to do a test for that and it's quite personal!"

"I'm an INTP," says Clare, "It's The Thinker:

logical, original, creative thinkers. Can become very excited about theories and ideas. Exceptionally capable and driven to turn theories into clear understandings. Highly value knowledge, competence, and logic. Quiet and reserved, hard to get to know well. Individualistic, having no interest in leading or following others."

"That's not a bad summary of you, " says Bigsy, "But my way is to send the person a 'tone burst' of information and see what I get back.. It's a quick way to determine if they know about something or are bluffing. Then I can calibrate them."

"You sound like an INTJ - The Scientist: Independent, original, analytical, and determined. Have an exceptional ability to turn theories into solid plans of action. Highly value knowledge, competence, and structure. Driven to derive meaning from their visions. Long-range thinkers. Have superior standards for their performance, and the performance of others. Natural leaders but will follow if they trust existing leaders." Clare is reading from a small chart pasted into her notebook.

"I'll take that," says Bigsy.

"I usually read the room to get sense of the person type. I break it into four types," says Jake, "Directors, biased for action, Thinkers - who are analytical, Relators - literally into relationships and Socialisers - who are the most spontaneous. You can even tell when they sit around table. What do they bring, how much do they assemble. I guess it comes with my journalist training."

"It looks as if we all have different techniques. What about you, Christina?"

She smiles and then offers, "Do they have a weapon? Can I body-throw them?" Enigmatic as ever.

Chuck returns us to the original topic. "I can email him, you know," says Chuck. "I'm sure Sike would be up for a call."

We are all smiling at Skookum.

Zoe Demelza

By the next day, Chuck and Christina are back in London. Chuck is on the trail of his ex-marine Navajo buddy Sike. He is going to set up a simple conference call between us all after he's made contact.

Meanwhile, Clare, Bigsy and I meet Zoe Demelza for coffee. She is the Exeter student who we had met at Jago and Emmanuelle's party. We remember she is studying for her master's and wants to do something with biological human-machine interfaces, but first is studying liberal arts as a precursor to machine ethics. A smart cookie who gave us a breakthrough moment in our last investigation.

We meet at Artigiano Espresso & Wine Bar, a trendy coffee place in Exeter near to John Lewis. Think pavement tables to watch the world (mainly shoppers and students with stretched bags of groceries).

Zoe arrives wearing a neat blue/grey suit jacket, grey knitted top, and blue jeans. I've seldom seen her out of the formal kitchen maid look from Jago's party. She's got her hair down too, which is a kind of straight chestnut brown. Her work at Magister Grange had been a way to earn extra cash, but back then we learned she was also assisting the local police in an investigation related to drug trafficking. Our last encounter neatly wrapped up that entire series of events.

"Hey," she hugs Clare and smiles sweetly to me and Bigsy, "Oh yes, I remember when we first met, Jake, I was coming back from the greenhouses with Robin Duggan and you were with Bianca Hart?"

We both smile and I remember she has a great memory. But then, I can still remember her sweaty story about being trapped in a door gap between rooms with Christopher Law, back in Magister Grange.

"I moved to a place in Exeter this year, still renting but a bigger house, and more room. I'm away from the student madness now, although there's other kinds here," she says, "And I'm no longer helping investigate drug rings for Penrose and Trewella. It's been nice to get my whole life back. Although I'm intrigued that you would want to ask me anything!"

"It's about Leonard Richards. Do you remember him from the party?" I ask.

"No, he wasn't there. I remember chatting to Penelope Richards and thinking she must be wealthy, owning those vineyards and all. I was most surprised when I discovered Penelope was married to the local vicar!"

"How would you describe Penelope?" asks Clare.

"Mild-mannered, pleasant. She had a fairly entitled attitude, although she was at ease talking to me as one of the hired help." Zoe smiles.

"Is this Penelope?" asks Clare, showing a photo.

"Oh no," answers Zoe, "the person in this picture looks like a villain from central casting. Penelope was far more restrained. And I suppose that man in the picture is her husband?" she looks a little longer at the picture.

"No, I can say I've never seen him before - he looks like Snape out of Potter. I'm intrigued, what's this all about?"

Clare answers, "To be honest, we don't know. They sent us down here to dig around."

"Well, let me know if I can help," says Zoe, she pauses, "And if there is fee earning potential, then count me in!"

At that moment, a graceful Chinese woman approaches us.

"Hey Zoe!"

"Hey Li Mei! - Everyone - this is Li Mei, my flat mate; oh - she also goes by the name Cathy Kwan - easier for Brits to say... These are some friends I know from when I worked at Magister Grange,"

"Zǎoshang hǎo! - Good Morning!"

"Don't be fooled by the Chinese, Li Mei has lived in Paris as well. She speaks perfect French as well as English."

"Neither are as hard as my Mother tongue," she says.

"And she's a mad background. Her mother was in a performing troupe, and taught Li Mei some of the moves."

"Yes, my mother was a Chinese trapeze artist," says Li Mei, "But there's not much call for those skills in Exeter."

"So, what are you doing?" I ask.

"Studying: robotics, just like Zoe. It's how we met."

"It's kind of weird and fortuitous all at once,"

says Zoe, "Li Mei didn't know many people when she moved to Exeter and was in the Halls. Then we met and I suggested she could help me share the house for her next year."

"I'm studying for a Masters," explains Li Mei, "It's been really helpful having Zoe sharing with me."

"And you three must be the Londoners that Zoe told me about. I can see that you have a tote bag from the Tate," she looks at Bigsy then she looks at me, "Your pen says, 'South Bank Centre'! You get up to any more adventures, you count me in!"

"You have a great eye for detail," observes Clare, introducing the three of us properly. "Would you like to join us for coffee?"

"Gotta bounce," says Li Mei, "I'm meeting Gabs in the Library," she glances further along the road, "But hey, it was nice to meet you all."

She waves and flitters softly away and we are all aware of how lightly she moves. Maybe she doesn't swing on trapezes, but the skills have certainly rubbed off.

Zoe, explains, "Em, Li Mei is one of my flatmates and Gabs - Daniel - is the other. Gabs is short for Gabor and is a nickname that Daniel Wendling inherited. He knows Li Mei from Paris, where he was a street performer."

"Interesting and colourful, but not a way to become rich," observes Bigsy.

"Oh no, Daniel is loaded," explains Zoe, "Some kind of family trust fund keeps him well oiled. But, you know, Li Mei and Daniel are best friends."

"But why the nickname?" asks Clare, intrigued.

Zoe answers, "Gab's street act is juggling and unicycle. But sometimes at festivals he'll perform a knife act. You know, throwing them."

"I thought that would be illegal?" says Bigsy.

"Ahah, I know about this from talking to Daniel," says Zoe, " His throwing knives are Category D weapons. That's, believe it or not, considered the least dangerous."

"I still don't get the nickname, though?"

"In a famous French movie, there's a knife thrower. His name is Gabor - Gabs - and is played by Daniel Auteil."

"Oh - La fille sur le pont? I love that movie," says Clare.

"Never seen it, " replies Bigsy.

"You must," says Zoe, and Clare nods her head.

Meanwhile, Christina had been chatting with her two Bulgarian flatmates, Desislava and Anelia in London. They had both realised that Christina was more than met the eye. A few days after we'd met Zoe, Christina invited them both to meet me and Chuck in a local pub on the banks of the River Thames. I let the train take the strain. Chuck met me at Paddington and we shared a cab to the pub.

Christina, Desislava and Anelia were all sitting together when we arrived. They were sharing a bottle of red wine.

"We knew it, " said Desi, "That Krasi was not a typical Bulgarian. We thought she was Russian."

Krasi. I wondered, then I remembered Christina was using her Bulgarian name Krasimira Radka. This would be difficult.

"So, are you British?" asked Anelia, looking confused. I nod and Chuck shakes his head. "I'm British and Chuck is American," I reply.

"We all trust one another?" asks Christina/Krasimira.

Desi and Anni nod. I can see this is another exciting moment in their lives. Chuck orders drinks for everyone from the bar.

We all sit around a big corner table. Christina orders another bottle. It's a really pleasant red. Robust with a hint of smoky barrel. I'm guessing it's from South America. Chuck looks approvingly at the bottle. "I may just take a photo," he says.

"Okay, you are not with the tax man or other authorities?" asks Anni, "And you know we came here the same way as you. Look, I don't want my residency to be messed up."

"Vizhte mili moi vsichki sme ot edna strana.," says Christina. I don't understand what she says but work out it is something placatory. They both lean back in their chairs.

"Vizhte, kazakh, che bŭlgarskiyat ĭ e malko neobichaen!" says Desi.

"They used to call us Russians kifla, when I was at the Akademy," smiles Christina, speaking in English.

"You speak pretty good Bulgarian actually, and you seem to know the slang!" observes Anni.

"Brat!" says Christina, "They used to think we'd be standing around being photographed next to the tanks and planes, not actually driving them... Oh - it's okay" - she looks over to Chuck, "Brat means 'Bro' in Bulgarian - and it's unisex."

Everyone laughs.

"But we worked out you were not native. You have a slightly unusual accent."

I work out that this will be Christina's 'Grand Reveal'.

Christina continues, "I was based at the The Vasil Levski National Military University right in the middle of Bulgaria. It was closer to Bucharest in Romania than it was to Sofia in Bulgaria and it was also over 200 twisty kilometres from Plovdiv, the main airport."

"Vasil Nevski - The Apostle of Freedom, a national hero of Bulgaria! But that Uni isn't a regular one? It was hardcore military!"

"So, you were at Veliko Tarnovo?" asked Anni, "My old boyfriend went there!"

"Small world," says Christina.

"I remember his special uniform. It made him look like a snowman!'

"That was the whites. White uniform with red

braid, and a white hat. The Presidential Guard uniform. We usually wore greens. The National Guard had a reverse colour uniform, with red jacket and white braiding."

"She passes the test," says Anni, looking at Desi, who nods, "So now you can ask us what you like?"

"Okay," says Christina. "We are trying to find out some more about how you got involved with this whole set-up?"

Anni begins, "Let's go back a while. You can imagine. We are economic migrants. Our families fell into debt with the wrong people. In fact, most of our village did. We decided to do something about it and found out about the Skövde thing. "

Desi takes over, "Skövde started in Sweden but would give people like us a way to recover the situation. We applied to Sweden but were informed that there was a similar scheme operating from the United Kingdom. First we were told about the Manston, Kent site operated by the UK Government. It was run by Prison Service contractors and was reputed to be awful. Weapons, overcrowding, diphtheria. Look at the UK statistics. 2018 and 2019 about 200-500 people crossed the channel by boat. Then in 2020 it rose to 10,000. 2021? 30,000. And then 2022 around 45,000. This Clyst Richards thing seemed to be a good alternative."

"But how did you qualify?" asks Chuck, "I mean it must be one in a thousand?"

"It was, but we were both well educated in Bulgaria," Desi says," I'm a Doctor and Anna was studying but is a Masters already. It's also how we acquired such good English."

"What disciplines?" asks Chuck.

Anni answers, "We both studied in Varna, a technical university. We were working with Power Systems mainly, but the education gave us a broader spectrum of knowledge."

"It was about utility power distribution but took into account the modelling of weather and its effects on power surges and their balancing."

Desi adds, "Yes, and it included the effects on infrastructure such as air traffic control and ways to manage blackouts and brownouts because of unpredicted events."

"Wow," I say, "It's a bit different from working in wine bars in London?"

Desi answers, "It is, but the payments because we were head-hunted to come here more than make up for it. We both have to work two and a half years in the UK and can then get on with our lives. The down payments for us to come here, the regular compensation and the end payments show both our families will be in the clear. And we'll have both BRPs (Biometric Residency Permits) and 'right to work' share codes.

"Share codes?" asks Chuck.

"Yes - in the UK we need these codes issued by the UK Government in order to work," explains Desi, " And somehow Reverend Richards seems to have a fast track."

"So, what are your extra duties over here in London?" asks Chuck, bluntly.

"We are supposed to listen and acquire intelligence about a joint project. It's called Project Awesome and is a combined US and British thing."

"Our wine bar is in a prime spot along the Thames, we get Americans from their Embassy, Secret Service types from SIS and our fair share of scientists from the sheds."

"The sheds?" asks Chuck. I'm glad it was him.

"Yes, those sheds behind the market - you know Nine Elms. It's full of boffins working on projects. They also come to the wine bar to unwind."

Calling Sike

Chuck has arranged the simple conference call. Voice only. Bigsy, Clare and I are together and Christina and Chuck dialled in from separate addresses in London.

I can see that Chuck is excited, "Hey Sike, long time eh?"

Sike replies, "Chuck! This is cool. Don't be a stranger! Bear Down!"

Chuck answers, "I put on the moccasins!"

"What! And it's not even August!"

"No matter, like I said in the email, I wanted to pick your brains about weather management."

"You know I'm lecturing on Climate Management at UArizona?"

"I know and it's a silly name, isn't it?"

"What? Climate Management?"

They both laugh. The rest of us introduce ourselves on the call. Sike sounds just like Chuck and not at all how I'd expected.

"Long version or short version?" he asks.

Chuck: "Well, some background and then the latest happening things?"

" 'K. Well, I'll start right back, but go fast. In the olden days, they used to think that gunfire caused rain to fall. Napoleon and American Civil War - big battles then rain. Then Texas trying to make storm rains. All hearsay results. Then we get to Wilhelm Reich - the first Cloudbuster - Kate Bush wrote a song about him."

Chuck looks at us for approval, says, "You see, I knew Sike would have some valuable input."

"Well, then fast forward to 2010. Abu Dhabi in the UAE claims to have created over 50 rainstorms, using seeding, just like we attempted, Chuck."

Chuck smiles.

Sike continues, "Then the Chinese created the Beijing Weather Modification Office. They used variants of silver iodide to create precipitation.

The only ill effect was yellow hands from handling it."

"As well as creating storms, there's the breakup of storms by splitting them into smaller units. Silver iodide again or - would you believe it - soot.
Anything that droplets can form around. The introduction of polymers caused it to change up a gear. Polyacrylic acid which can absorb 1500 times its weight of water."

"Hmm, not so good for other environmental reasons?" muses Clare.

Sike answers, "Yes, you are right, but compared with the storm damage, I'm guessing the initial impact from polymers was minor. Then they scaled it up. 9000lbs was dropped from a high-altitude B-57 bomber into a storm system."
"NASA plane," interjects Chuck. Sike nods.

"Did it work?" asks Clare.

"Reportedly," answers Sike, "It's well documented, but National Oceanic and Atmospheric Administration cancelled the programme. Politics. Well, they had their other ideas and were 'well-funded'."

"The other ideas?" asks Chuck.

"The administration went a little mad," explains Sike,"But they could pay military contractors handsomely. We saw lasers used to discharge lightning in storms, pouring liquid nitrogen onto the sea to deprive hurricanes of heat energy, and using soot to absorb sunlight and change air temperature and create convection currents in the outer wall of a hurricane."

"Any of it work?" asks Chuck, "It's after my time but seems to be like more of the same."

"Oh, it was, just better funded," answers Sike, "Like the wind turbine ideas, which were a copy of the old times hail cannons, designed to blow energy into the atmosphere to disperse hurricanes before they make landfall."

Clare asks, "Do you know who supported it? Which contractors?"

Sike answers, "No afraid not, although I expect it was the usual suspects. However, the US more or less abandoned these experiments until it got wind of what the Russians and Chinese were developing. Oh, I should mention that none of what I'm mentioning is classified, by the way."

Chuck nods, "So I take it there is more?" He can read Sike so well.

"Well, Semper Supra!" says Sike, "Always above."

"What? The US Space Force?" asks Chuck.

"Let's call it the next generation," says Sike, "Post 9/11, when the Space Corps became the Space Force. Courtesy of Donald Trump. Now it's got eight and a half thousand military employees."

Christina chips in, "Of course the Russians established the Space Troops in 1955, and then the Russian Space Forces in 1992."

"Agreed, but they didn't amount to much," says Sike, "...Well, except for their Intercontinental Ballistic Missiles."

"Hardly stealth weapons!" says Chuck.

"That's the thing," says Sike, "We've seen a couple of interesting occurrences. My first example is from the sea of Okhotsk. That's north-east of Japan alongside Sakhalin Island. You know the long island that looks like an extension of Japan but is purely Russian."

"Oh yes," says Clare, "An oil rich area with plenty of ice floes."

"Yes," says Sike, "Well, on this occasion a Russian trawler went down. The radio reported unexpectedly freak weather conditions.
A whirlpool swallowed the trawler amidst storm waves reaching 15 meters (50 feet) in height.

It started without even a weather warning."

"Could it have been generated?" asks Chuck.

"We don't know," replies Sike, "But then there was a second similar occurrence near to the Marshall Islands. This time it was a container ship. Also, Russian. It reported sudden sea swell and promptly capsized. Radio reports described 40-foot waves and a huge eddy current. It was from nothing to a major storm in about a minute. We have weather reports from the area at the time this one occurred."

"The thing is," says Chuck, "Even with our bombers and the iodine, it would still take time for a storm to manifest."

"Exactly," says Sike, "Which makes me think this was caused another way."

Flying to Corsica

It wasn't difficult to work out why Corsica wasn't on holidaymaker lists. The flight from Exeter took 13 hours. It was a two or maybe three-hour direct flight, but we had to go first to Amsterdam and then on to Corsica, after a ten-hour layover. At least we'd decided to go in number, and so Chuck, Bigsy Clare and I all took the journey.

We'd be in a hotel in Bastia, but to be honest, it looked like a strange area on the maps, at least.

And when we arrived, the taxi took us the short distance to the hotel along the waterfront, but it looked like one huge ferry terminal and car park. Not the chic beauty of, say, Cannes or Nice, instead it reminded me of the car ferry port at Calais.

Then past the pink walled entrance into the hotel. It seemed to be a green side door, but I could tell it was the main entrance. It somehow looked different from the picture on our booking. Then to our rooms. 'Some rooms include a private bathroom,' it proudly discloses. And the rooms had a sea view once we'd got to them via the small elevator. Although there seemed to be a bit of noisy work going on in the street outside our rooms.

We shouldn't be staying in Bastia long.

We sit on the balcony to observe the sea, across from the car terminal. The men working are keen on using hammers and a loud machine that makes a kind of repetitive clang that techno sound engineers would spend hours trying to create in software.

"We'd better check with Zoe on the likelihood we can use ask Li Mei to help us," says Clare.

I sense she is trying to distract us from thinking about our hotel surroundings and the incessant building works.

Clare calls Zoe, who picks up straight away. Clare is chatting to Zoe, awaiting the inevitable question about the background noise. I sense when it comes, and it gives Clare a chance to utter, "Yes I'm in a hotel in Bastia, Corsica right now."

I can hear some kind of fast banter from Zoe, and see Clare is smiling.

"Look Zoe, you know your friend, Li Mei? She said she'd be keen to work with us, do you think she meant it? ...Is she? ...Oh yes please...No, we won't need her in Corsica."

I sense I'm picking up one side of the conversation which had Zoe in the middle and Li Mei at the far end.

Then Clare's tone changes. "Yes...Yes... We'll be back in a couple of days. Of course. No, you'll be perfectly safe."

Clare is talking directly now to Li Mei. I take that as a good sign.

"Yes I'm in his room right now, but no we're not. It's easiest to confer this way.... Yes...I will...Zoe has my number and contact details...I think we'll be back in a couple of days...Oh yes... Yes... Definitely! Ciao Ciao,"

Clare grins back at me, "Li Mei is pleased to work with us. She is treating the whole thing as an adventure. She asked if she could come to Corsica!"

Good. A plan is beginning to form.

Marie-Louise Deschanel

The next morning, we are meeting Marie-Louise Deschanel for brunch at Café des Gourmets, a five-minute walk from our pink hotel. The cafe outside looks unassuming, with a row of street-side tables and a faded red awning. Inside through the building there's a green space at the back, where we are meeting Marie-Louise.

The brunch menu is all les œufs à la bénédictine, les œufs à la florentine, la brioche perdue aux fruits rouges, la tartine crémière… Que des classiques de votre maison du brunch. Marie-Louise has done well with this suggested venue.

She arrives at the restaurant looking the epitome of French elegance. Black leather jacket, unstructured blue shirt, tied in a large knot at the front. Light tailored slacks, white sneakers with a light blue V motif, and a colourful foulard around her neck. She's carrying a tote bag from Rue d'Artiste (Of course she is!). She moves like she's in a movie. Oh, and did I mention the smile.

Clare beams back at her. "Loving the Veja!" she says, looking at Marie-Louise's feet.

"These sneakers," smiles Marie-Louise, "Have seen things!"

We all introduce ourselves and I'm aware that other cafe occupants are looking at us. We are the cool table.

"We're trying to work out if there is something dubious here in Corsica," begins Clare, "Thank you for agreeing to see us."

Marie-Louise starts, "I guess you are all new to Corsica, so I'll start with a little introduction. You might expect Corsica to be at the forefront of self-promotion but it's all a lot more low key."

We all nod at this. A crime centre with tourists. Okay.

She continues, "Some years ago, Corsica may have suffered from an image problem, because of the mafia, but now that's all in the past. Okay, the old mafia stories were down to the internal squabbles of wider banditry and absolutely did not affect visitors. The FLNC also often hit the headlines and so for some years contributed to that bad reputation.

"Yes, these stories of banditry are part of Corsican history and our strong character, but our island has always been a truly peaceful haven for our visitors, who can enjoy the island's charm and beauty in complete security."

As she is saying this, I'm acutely aware that her lawyer father was assassinated.

'The whole of Corsica has a morality that differs from elsewhere – everybody is involved to a greater or lesser extent in crime, whether it's just cheating the French state or something more serious."

She is edgy. I can sense that she's not entirely on the legal side of things.

"The reason is that Corsica has never been allowed to develop into a civilisation running its own affairs – it has always been dominated by outsiders – Genoese, North Africans, even, for a short time after the Revolution, the British."

She smiles as she looks at us. British.

'Then, under the British, Corsica developed democracy, under Pasquale Paoli. Indeed, Paoli is fondly remembered by his statue, dominating the main square in the mountain town of Corte, the only one of the various historic capitals on the island chosen by the Corsicans themselves.

"The democracy lasted a short time until the French came in," Marie-Louise says, "Corsica has never been allowed to run its own affairs so it's never been allowed to develop into a proper civilised state – it's always been every man for himself."

She is very self-assured and eloquent and speaks like a well-spoken Londoner. It is almost familiar.

"The newspapers say that Corsica's salaries were the lowest of any département in France, yet they say Corsicans saved more than anyone else.

"That's the proof that there is a hell of a lot of cash but a lot of dodgy, dodgy stuff – a lot of drugs, etcetera, all tied up with organised crime in the south of France."

She sees me noticing her English accent. Nothing I said, just the way I smiled at certain words.

"I was married to an Englishman. Nigel, a gangster type. Small time south London until he was arrested. He is still in prison in Belmarsh, south London."

I ask, "Belmarsh? That's for more serious incidents, isn't it?"

She answers, "Jeffrey Archer was there, also

Julian Assange. In the interests of full disclosure Nigel's in a single occupancy cell, but he is doing time to pay off a debt."

I consider. The 'small time' and his sentence don't seem in balance.

I ask cautiously, "What was he arrested for?"

"Jewellery theft, the police accused him of being a member of the Pink Panther gang. It's a real thing, the police named it after that movie. I know he wasn't involved. Most of his stuff was low-level crime. Goods being fenced, that kind of thing. The gang knew him though and asked him to confess. They needed someone who didn't know anything to spend some time inside. They paid him very well. Not surprising - they have stolen about £350 million of jewels over multiple robberies."

So how is it you are here?" asks Clare.

"I fell in love with a boy," says Marie-Louise, "In London. I know, it sounds corny, but Nigel was then a dashing man-about-town, with a daring edge. I guess I liked the wrong sort of men. And he liked me because I was French and a little exotic to him, " she smiles wryly.

"We fell in love, were married at Kensington Registry Office and had two beautiful years together. Then the squeeze came, and he was forced into the set-up. He'd borrowed money and was now in debt to the wrong crowd."

"One day, there was a knock on the door. Four big holdalls of mixed large denomination cash were left, which he moved to a lockup garage in Woolwich, ironically only a stone's throw from the prison."

I'm thinking that it must have been drug money. Loose banknotes. My quick calculation is that three holdalls can hold a million pounds.

"The next day, another knock on the door. This time, it was the police. Nigel had been told what to say and was arrested, tried, and later sentenced. Of course we had all this payoff money in holdalls. I knew enough to be able to get it to Corsica, where I could call in a few favours and get it converted into bank accounts. He's always insisted it's 50:50 between us and so there's still two large deposits waiting for his release. I had to pay dearly to get it laundered."

"He went to Belmarsh because it is surprisingly secure. We agreed to divorce and for me to take back my unmarried name. For him there was little chance of mishaps, especially as he is single occupancy. He says it's like he has to work abroad for a few years to raise money for our future."

"Will you re-marry?" asks Clare.

"No! We can still be the best kind of

companions, but don't need to draw attention to ourselves."

"Why are you telling us all this?" asks Bigsy.

"Well, I want you to trust me, and I think the truth is a sign of that," she answers.

"But now, based upon my story, you can see how Corsica gets used. And many get away with it because there are lots of Corsicans in the judiciary and the civil service. They just lose any documents so that, if you have a Corsican name, you will not get prosecuted."

"Today, bullet holes in French road signs and occasional scrawled graffiti are the only reminders of the violence of the FLNC, and a cynic might wonder why the French state should worry too much about the fate of 300,000 people who don't like it and are geographically closer to Italy."

Bigsy had pointed out the bullet holes on the way to our meeting.

"Perhaps the reason it should worry is that Provence-Alpes Maritimes-Côte d'Azur – with 0.3 murders per 10,000 people in 2018 – now runs Corsica's 0.34 a close second. The link with organised crime across both regions is self-evident."

I look around and although we are the coolest

table, I can see several others with symbols of wealth. Fancy watches, discreet jewellery, supermodel looks, a casually tossed Ferrari keyring.

Marie-Louise continues, "If you look around the streets of Ajaccio, there are too many luxury cars for the relatively small official financial output of the island. It's organised crime, of course."

We all nod. A smile flickers across her face.

"These gangsters are relatively untouchable but making large investments in property both in Corsica and all across Europe. New Apartment blocks are laundered money at rest. Investigations so far have been limited to the crimes themselves, and not on the source of the vast amounts of dirty cash they are handling."

"But are you worried about your own transactions?" asks Clare.

"Not at all, mine were done a couple of years ago. The banks in question have all been reversed into other banks. Now I'm with totally legitimate finance houses. It's what I paid a premium for."

"But if you can do this, then surely the French State can too? You know, follow the money around." Bigsy looks perplexed.

"Money can oil things or gum them up,"

answers Marie-Louise, "The French state can play a much bigger role in helping to solve Corsica's problems – not by putting more policemen on the streets, but by giving resources so that the money side of the criminal activity can be properly investigated. Instead, the money goes into block and tackling any investigations."

We've finished the brunch and the sleek waitress asks if we'd like anything else.

Without thinking, Marie-Louise orders a Pernod. We all order the same. I secretly wonder if the other tables will copy us - the cool table.

"Let's talk about why we are here," says Chuck.

"I think I know," answers Marie-Louise, "It's about the Calvets, isn't it?"

"How do you know?" asks Clare.

"Bonifacio," says Marie-Louise, "One of the biggest moves into Bonifacio, was by Renee Calvet, and then a few weeks later a Corporation buys the property next door. My guess? The total value would be something like €35 million. Everyone will have noticed it. The high-net-worth part of Corsica gets two huge property deals adjacent to one another."

I'm impressed. Marie-Louise is very astute.

"Which Corporation?" asks Bigsy. We already know the answer.

"Brant Industrie," says Marie-Louise. Three cherries on the slot machine.

"Brant also bought the nearby luxury hotel. And they are getting the road access upgraded as well."

I hear the clunks. Now its three crowns on the slot machine.

Technical Debt

"You know about my father?" asks Marie-Louise, "François Deschanel. A lawyer. He was murdered. Broad daylight. An Ajaccio filling station. Gunned down by 10 bullets from an automatic pistol by a motor bike passenger."

"Our condolences. There is nothing we can say.," says Clare, intensely.

"It's why I'll help you now," says Marie-Louise, "But you must know the danger. Here it is organised crime. They like it here because it is hidden away. People talk about South America, Pakistan, Turkey, The Caymans. Even Sicily, but seldom Corsica."

We nod, "Different crime too," says Clare.

"America helped a lot of it," says Marie-Louise, "Improvements to infrastructure make it all possible. My father had been investigating. Beneath the open markets that facilitate global trade and manufacturing lies a less tangible network of intellectual property and technological expertise. This provides American leaders with unparalleled levers of control. Well strictly, my father found it was because of a certain enabling corporation. A company called Brant, which was an offshoot of the well-known Raven Corp."

None of us look very surprised. It seems to be a recurring theme.

"These world-spanning systems were not created as part of a deliberate plot for political domination. They were mostly built by private companies like Brant pursuing efficiency and profit. These modern empires have turned the subterranean machineries that enable global markets and information flows—fibre-optic cables, server farms, financial payment systems, and the manufacturing systems that produce complex products such as semiconductors—into tools of coercion.

"My father's note show that just like EDS used to run the American intelligence systems from a huge server farm in Plano, Texas, now lower profile systems make new hubs spread carefully around the world. "

"Bigsy nods, "Check out Data Centre Alley or look for Coreweave and you'll still find vast amounts of citizen data being processed. It's still in Texas, but around Dallas now."

Marie-Louise reaches into her leather strap handled tote bag, pulls out a binder with some papers.

"This is what my father was working on when he was killed. He describes the technical debt of certain banking systems. They cut corners to get ahead. It was like a guilty secret. The main system builders. You guessed it. Brant."

Bigsy adds, "I should explain. Technical debt is neither good nor bad, it's debt. And just like financial debt, there are several schools of thought around whether technical debt is a good or bad thing."

"Oh, it is bad for a banking system," answers Marie-Louise, "unless you are criminals. It's a just a polite way of saying that corners have been cut."

Bigsy explains, "Most software companies like Brant are under pressure from the market and competitive forces to develop and ship fast. This need for speed leads many product and software development teams to make the trade-off between taking on technical debt or launching later."
Clare asks, "One could mention the UK's own sketchy Horizon system- it took twenty years to be found out."

"It's more than what Bigsy describes; sometimes

it's deliberate corner and done to remove checks and balances," says Marie-Louise,

Bigsy nods, " Yes, technical staff often try to explain technical debt to business staff, who may not immediately see the implications. The main issue seems to be that, unlike financial debt, technical debt is much less visible, and so people have an easier time ignoring it."

"It's what my father discovered, in the course of his normal investigations," explains Marie-Louise, "These banking systems were intentionally designed with loopholes. Loopholes through which money could be poured. At a casual glance, these systems seem simultaneously dull and arcane. The boring and complicated wiring and plumbing arrangements of the global economy.

"But Brant understands that the plumbing is political. Just as all roads once led to Rome, the world's fibre-optic networks, financial systems, and semiconductor supply chains converge on the United States, allowing it to project its might."

Bigsy adds, "So there we have it. A banking system designed for criminals."

François Deschanel

Chuck speaks uncharacteristically softly, "We will need to meet the man who owns the link to the processes. To attract him, we can use what your father discovered. Look at this:"

Chuck eyes the papers that Marie-Louise has produced. It is her father's notes:

"New technologies and market freedoms are about to decentralise power, rendering once vital strategic choke points irrelevant, and shifting the tectonic plates of national sovereignty.

"Global flows of information, money, and trade are not only flooding across national borders but washing them away, creating a true global marketplace in which agile individuals and businesses could evade government regulation. This is how Corsica fits in."

Chuck adds: "More significantly, it's how Brant

fits in. But François Deschanel speaks and writes of the irresistible challenges that global information technology and markets pose to government power long before others were really paying attention."

Clare agrees, " Yes. Financial flows were once largely restricted by national borders, and the Internet was originally an obscure government-funded experiment. Before social media and the consequent social engineering appeared, it wasn't clear that technology would transform everything. And now we can add Artificial Intelligence into the mix."

Bigsy adds, "Everyone is pretending they thought of it first and have the best models. The big secret they all know is they are all based on copied algorithms and work the same way. Marketing, as usual, wins the battle."

Marie-Louise adds, "My father was a full-time lawyer seeking the truth and justice. He wasn't an academic or a think-tank president. He wrote his thoughts from the perspective of a participant in the growing global financial marketplace where he was engaging in polite and perhaps ironic understatement. I know, it's not solely a British thing."

She continues, "The histories of globalisation pay close attention to the politicians and high officials who cleared the way for open markets, and the thinkers who argued for them, but they regularly ignore the business leaders and crime lords who actually built them."

Clare nods, "Yes, I can see that. Look closely at the burgeoning of international finance, of information networks, of the logistical innovations that transformed trade. His descriptions are all about the high seas of global markets, watching certain corporations out-sail nation states and create their own free and leveraged republics."

"By certain corporations you are talking about Brant?" asks Bigsy.

"And a handful of others. The usual suspects you might say," answers Marie-Louise.

Flight back

The flight back is routed differently. We have to go to Marseilles and then London. We decide to stop off at Amanda's offices, on the South Bank. It's also a chance for us to pick up some different clothes before we head back to Exeter. More Seasalt than Urban Outfitters.

"I'm going into the office," announces Bigsy.

"It'd be a shame not to tell Christina we are here in London," says Clare.

"It's settled then," I say, "We'll go to where Christina works."

By the next day we've called Chuck and we make our way to Christina's riverside bar. We know that we'll be meeting with Amanda tomorrow, but this gives us all a chance to straighten our facts.

Christina's bar is on the outskirts of the stylish

area that has grown around Battersea Power Station. They have been building there for ages, and the entire environment is now looking complete. We've all hugged one another and settle into a conversation about our situation. Christina's bar is terminally colourful and hip. Lifestyle prints on the walls of women in curious poses with boots balanced upon their heads. Other playfully oriented ones of men in riding outfits and chequered clothing. Everyone drinking cocktails. Christina, grinning, brings a big tray of Cosmopolitans and Old Fashions towards us.

Clare speaks first, "We know that the set up in Exeter is simply the tip of an iceberg. That the Reverend Richards is some kind of front."

Bigsy adds, "And there's plenty of funding for all of this."

I add," With Brant somehow in the back of things."

Christina distributes the drinks and suggests, "The system they are setting up is about control. It goes well beyond a single theme. It looks like underground infrastructure, ground level finance and then aerial climate management."

"There are some pieces missing," suggests Bigsy, "That's why they need to gather further intel."

"Something to do with climate," suggests

Chuck, "Those moves around Exeter, it's linked to Meteorological Office systems."

"Same here in London," adds Christina, "Those tin sheds behind the Covent Garden Market are all R&D facilities. Weather research. It's also close to the U.S. London embassy scene."

"Not so far from that old listening station we found either," says Bigsy, "When Brant were trying to lobby Members of Parliament."

"So, we can infiltrate the process, to work out what is happening," says Christina, "But it will take obshchak-sized amounts of cashflow."

"That's what we need to ask Amanda. She can source the money and hand it to us, but only for two or three weeks, I'd guess."

Chuck nods, "That's how long we'd have to get this thing solved,"

"But what's our back-story," asks Christina, "How are we generating so much free cash?"

"Will they care?" asks Chuck, "As long as they get to process it."

"Somehow we need to put up a front person. Untraceable. Accompanied by a couple of us. Christina and Chuck, I'd imagine." says Clare.

"You bet, " says Christina. Chuck nods.

"Ideally it should be someone who doesn't look the part," says Christina, "Makes it more plausible."

"Vancouver: Chinese money laundering," suggests Clare, "It's a big deal nowadays."

"No, move it to France, " says Bigsy. I realise what Bigsy is thinking. An unknown Chinese front, living in Paris.

Clare speaks, "Do you think we could persuade Zoe's friend to be a part of it?"

"As well as Li Mei, Amanda will be the one to ask," says Bigsy, "and we'll need to build up a story."

"Tomorrow then, we'll ask Amanda for £5 million and a set of fake papers for a Zoe's friend Li Mei so that she can bait the trap."

What could possibly go wrong?

Fishing

I have laid aside business and gone a-fishing.

Of which, if thou be a severe, sour-complexioned man, then I here disallow thee to be a competent judge.

Angling may be said to be so like the mathematics that it can never be fully learnt.

Izaak Walton The Compleat Angler 1653-1655

Bait for a deal

We are with Amanda in her Vauxhall Cross office again. Clare, Chuck, Bigsy, Christina, Grace, and myself. I'm prepared for how this discussion can end.

Chuck begins, "Okay, so we need to create a situation. Something that will attract their attention."

"Money needs to be at the root," says Clare.

"More than that. A regular large supply of money," adds Bigsy.

"I can help with that," says Amanda.

"What would you need as a run-rate to get attention?" asks Grace.

"At least £5 million. £5 million a week." says Chuck, "Or roughly an annual turnover of a quarter of a billion US Dollars."

"Okay, that's a lot. It will limit how long this can run," says Amanda.

"But we must be trying to catch some pretty big fish," says Bigsy, "I mean, the Sinaloa drug cartel is around a $3 billion annual turnover."

"But what are they doing?" asks Clare, " We still don't really know."

"Its war without gunsmoke," says Christina, "They are manipulating the environment to their advantage. It's three layered."

Christina continues, "Underground - the comms network of the world. Tapped into and monitored. Surface level - the economic processes and the management of borders. Above in the sky - the manipulation of the environment. Eco-warfare."

"Do those things for long enough and you'd get control of the planet, " says Chuck.

Christina adds, "It's what STORMBREW was about. Unremarkable coloured lines connecting the Americas, Europe, and Africa, heading to the margins en route to Asia and Australia."

Grace adds, "Edward Snowdon discovered it. The map's title: STORMBREW: and more acronyms than you can shake a stick at."

"So, who knows about this?" asks Bigsy.

Grace replies, "Everyone in intelligence since the Snowden expose. Almost no-one before it and hardly anyone else still knows about it because there are so many other juicy lines to pursue. Things like caller info harvesting - who talks to whom. Like PRISM which scrapes the servers of major US service providers such as YouTube, Skype, Google, and Apple. All subsequently denied, of course.

"Well, wouldn't you deny everything?" asks Clare, smiling.

Grace continues, "Then there's one which I think Bigsy will like: Boundless Informant is a tool that allows the NSA to compile and track the metadata it collects around the world. A 'global heat map' sorts the intelligence sources by country, type, and volume, allowing quick analysis of which countries are most targeted, as well as when the information was gathered."

"I knew of Boundless Informant, I have just never heard it confirmed," says Bigsy.

Grace adds, "One that's no great surprise to anyone is the allegations that the NSA has been hacking mainland Chinese and Hong Kong computers since 2009.

"And vice-versa?" asks Clare.

"No comment," says Grace.

"Ask yourselves who wins the contracts to provide many of these functions," says Amanda.

"Surely not Brant?" asks Clare.

"Collect the prize," says Grace, " Or more precisely, Brant has a prize worth claiming...access to the world's secrets."

"But didn't GCHQ get found out after the hacks to the G20 members, " says Bigsy, "British GCHQ officials could obtain real-time listings of calls made by targeted persons and read their emails without notice."

Clare adds, "And I remember that GCHQ seemed to be able to hack a bunch of communications using a system called Tempora."

"Yes, but it was temporary data and always 'after the fact'," says Grace, "Great to analyse what already happened but less useful at predicting events in advance."

"This spying business seems very leaky" I observe.

"It can be but think of the volumes of data being handled. You have to know what to look for," adds Grace. "And ideally have a map."

She continues, "Cue STORMBREW! Maps don't

just depict physical locations. They make them understandable, turning complex physical geography into a subset of essential features—power, territory, authority, reach. Every map of any country of the world condenses the long, bloody history that created its borders. But maps don't just represent physical space. They can revise boundaries according to the priorities of the mapmakers, laying down sovereign claims over where one country's laws start and others end."

Bigsy adds, "That is why maps have long been a tool of empire. Since the 1400s when Pope Alexander issued a decree that chopped the world in half. The pope said a line be drawn across the globe, stretching from the North Pole to the South, one hundred leagues west and south of the Azores and Cape Verde Islands. Alexander declared that all territories past that line belonged to the kings of Spain and Portugal. This legal map defined the New World as a nobody's land, whose native peoples had no rights to rule or govern themselves and no redress beyond whatever the rulers of the Iberian Peninsula chose to bestow on them.

"Other rulers drew up their own maps in competition. The strange wizard John Dee was Queen Elizabeth I's court astrologer and is believed to have coined the term 'British Empire.' He believed that angels spoke to his crystal ball, disclosing the hidden secrets of the world.

"Dee also drew up exquisite maps, which he combined with laborious legal arguments to defend Queen Elizabeth's claims over the countries of the New World, asserting that they were rediscovered lands that had once been ruled from King Arthur's Camelot."
"You wait, Drake's Bay will become a thing," observes Clare.

Grace adds, "Superficially, the NSA map appears no more than a depiction of a technical project for acquiring information. STORMBREW was one of the NSA's many surveillance programs put in place after the attacks of September 11, 2001, capturing information from international cable traffic that crossed the United States. The NSA is perhaps the least well understood member of the U.S. intelligence community. Formally responsible for SIGINT - "Signal" intelligence, it is tasked with sifting the billions of daily global clicks, emails, and phone calls for useful strategic information."

"That is where these focal points or choke points come into their own," explains Bigsy. You can't tap into fibre optics like you can into copper wires. Instead, you need a prism to split the signal. Half for its intended purpose and half to go to the security community."

Grace smiles, "Exactly. The map depicts International 'Choke Points," inside the United

States, with the code names Breckenridge, Tahoe, Sunvalley, Whistler, Maverick, Copper Mountain, and Millington. Basically, any ski resorts you can think of in North America.

"Each of these choke points is located at a cable landing site or a switch in the Internet backbone. Like John Dee, the U.S. government desperately wanted to uncover the world's hidden secrets. However, the NSA didn't have to converse with angels via crystal balls. Instead, it just had to ask its STORMBREW corporate partner to sieve the data flowing through the Internet backbone for nuggets of precious and actionable information."

We all smile wryly. We can see where this is leading.

Grace continues, "Programs like STORMBREW provided the NSA with upstream access to floods of information flowing through telecommunications networks. Other programs, such as PRISM, enabled it to demand downstream data, which was more narrowly targeted and better organized, from big information technology companies.

She looks around at us, "Of course whenever the NSA received anything new, the other lucky recipients were - you've guessed it - Brant. Nor was the NSA the only U.S. agency discovering new worlds. Shortly after September 11, 2001, the U.S. Treasury Department started to map the apparent chaos of the world's financial system, using its new knowledge to spy on enemies and eventually cut them out of the global economy. An astonishingly complex reality could be reduced into something that was both graspable and tractable lines on a page, supplied courtesy of Brant."

"The choke points," breathes Chuck.

Grace nods, "Exactly, over time, these choke points allowed the U.S. to cut off businesses and even entire countries from access to the key global networks that wove the world's economy together.

Grace speaks, "Like the pope's map half a millennium before, the STORMBREW map and its equivalents don't just simplify the world. They turn the blank parts of the globalised economy into a territory that the United States can dominate, ably supported by Brant."

Amanda speaks, "It's the other way around. Brant is the top dog, in these arrangements; above nation states."

"Now this will sound weird, but there's something else, " says Clare, " We need some papers for a friend,"

"Who is that?" asks Grace.

"A friend of Zoe Demelza, living in Exeter and

with the name of Li Mei."

Grace pauses a moment; She is tapping into her keyboard.

Grace says, "I'm just running a quick search for Li Mei. She is well-known in China."

Clare asks, "Are you sure? It's not a common name like 'Smith' is it?"

"No. It shows her as a student in Exeter University. Studying Machine Learning. She sometimes goes by the name of Cathy Kwan."

Grace stares intently at her laptop screen.

"It says she is the daughter of a one-time theatrical performer and now has a stepfather Ren Mei who owns a satellite dish technology company. Dieshikeji. It means 'dish technology'. They changed the name to Quánbān zu" yōu, which is a subtle flex on the original name, apparently. It means 'best in class.'

Bigsy replies, "Quanban?" I know them. Tech gear, comms, dishes, transmitters, they say the founder is a genius."

Grace answers, "Well, his daughter Li Mei is a bit of a rebel, by all accounts. She left Chengdu, Sichuan to be brought up and schooled in Paris. Her mother's first husband was a former deputy secretary of East China Military and

Administrative Committees and deputy provincial governor of Sichuan.

"After her parents divorced, she adopted her mother's surname Kwan and kept it when her mother re-married a younger business man, the founder and owner of the tech company. They lived in Paris where Li Mei studied at SCAI (The Sorbonne Center of Artificial Intelligence) as Cathy Kwan, although her stepfather Ren Mei often travelled to China, visiting the corporate headquarters or one of the high-tech factories.

Then, suddenly, Ren Mei was collared for bank and wire fraud regarding financial transactions in violation of U.S. sanctions against Iran. A subsidiary of his company had functioned as Quanban's Iran-based subsidiary. Her father settled for a plea bargain to resolve the case through a deferred prosecution agreement. It's when Li Mei changed her name to Cathy Kwan, left Paris and came to Exeter to continue her robotics and AI study.

So, Li Mei is pretty smart and with a well-heeled background?" says Bigsy.

Grace continues reading, "Oh yes, and she's a long-term boyfriend Daniel Wendling. He's an equally well-heeled French citizen - his father is something big in the car industry. Cathy Kwan and Daniel Wendling appeared in all the society papers as an item at Le Bal des Débutantes in Paris shortly before they both left. Think heels, tiaras and haute couture gowns."

"What? For Daniel?" asks Bigsy.

"Yes, for Daniel to admire," snipes Clare.

"You remember? Li Mei was just going to meet Daniel in Exeter that time we all met at that coffee place," says Clare, " And Li Mei was definitely up for 'adventure'.

The Story for Leonard

"We need to work the situation up into a story," says Chuck.

"Simply that Li Mei has Chinese connections and needs to 'process' a lot of cash," says Clare.

"Wait a minute," says Bigsy, "Has Li Mei agreed to be involved with any of this?"

Clare nods, " I asked her whilst we were in Bastia. She is very keen."

Chuck says, "Christina can seed the conversation with Leonard Richards. That Li Mei has been the subject of a Suspicious Activity Report. We can say it is linked to her stepfather Ren Mei and the Quanban company."

Christina says, "All the more realistic because Ren Mei has been caught handling money from Quanban, then detained on bank and wire fraud and getting off through a plea bargain. If he's caught again he'd be liable for a long stretch inside."

Clare adds, "Leonard, being a vicar, is an ideal person to seek advice from. Except the advice is bait to draw him in. We'll get Christina and Zoe to visit the Reverend and set the lure."

Bigsy asks, "But will Christina or Zoe admit anything?"

"I think we can let the good vicar draw his own conclusions," says Christina, "And I think we know a couple of good men and true who could help us in that."

"A man and a woman," corrects Clare.

We smile at one another. Our old allies Detective Chief Inspector Morwen Penrose and Detective Inspector Tristan Trewella. They had been involved in the investigations at Magister Grange, although somehow missed the main plot last time.

Money Laundering

Clare had arranged for us to see our two friends in the Constabulary at the Police Headquarters in Exeter. Amanda had pulled some strings to arrange the appointment, liaising with the acting Chief Constable.

"The previous Chief has been under something of a cloud, for alleged misconduct," explains Clare.

"Wowsers!" utters Bigsy as we pull up to the new complex, "This is quite something! - It's better than New Scotland Yard!"

The two main buildings look imposing. White, with vertical windows, they create a kind of 'Jail' impression as we approach. I'm sure it was an architect's flourish.

We walk through the very light main reception area and I notice the theme of teal coloured panelling. Very Miami Vice.

We checked in. "This is amazing!" says Clare to the receptionist. "You should see the detention centre," smiles the receptionist, "Better than some local hotels.' Although this is a big site and there are other buildings too!"

We ask for Penrose and Trewella and are soon escorted to a small room where we will meet them.

The door opens and they both appear. I think DCI Morwen Penrose is about to hug us.

She doesn't.

They both shake our hands and then DI Trewella speaks, "Hello. We had another call from your well-connected associate Amanda Miller. She was most insistent that we meet you about this new situation that you are covering."

"We had no idea you worked in such an amazing location," says Clare, "This is like a corporate headquarters."

"Ironically, it is where we keep the prisoners awaiting trial - the main building is the custody suite," answers DCI Penrose.

"Well, I hope we can put our bumpy past behind us now," says Clare, "I know it wasn't all plain sailing with that business at Magister Grange."

"Life moves on," says Penrose, "Although it was a landmark occasion, what with murder, snipers, helicopters, the secret service. Not a typical case."

"We've the second lowest crime rate in the U.K.," says Penrose, "So that Magister Grange case rocked the boat somewhat."

We all smile.

You know that moment when people settle back in their chairs, more relaxed in the conversation? It happened just then. I'm sure Penrose and Trewella noticed as well.

"So, what's this about?" asks Penrose, as she stares at me.

"Okay, it's a further look at the drug trade around this area," I answer, "We think there may be money laundering."

"We've been investigating this forever," says Penrose, "I think the closest we came was that last caper of yours!"

"Okay, but this time we have a front man," I say.

"Oh yes, can I ask who?" asks Trewella.

Clare answers, "The Reverend Leonard Richards."

A pause.

"No, it can't be. He is such a well-respected man in this area. So much work for charity, for economic migrants. I think you've made a mistake, " answers Penrose.

"Exactly," says Bigsy, "A person you'd be least likely to suspect, hiding in plain sight."

"What proof do you have?" asks Trewella.

"None, yet. It's why we are running this assignment," I answer.

"Is that why Ms Miller is involved?" asks Penrose.

"Yes, it is. This situation is bigger than simply Devon," answers Clare.

"We think they are using the charity as a clearing house for illicit funds."

"What, money laundering?" asks Trewella.

"Exactly, but also running an even bigger scam. This could be large for both of you," says Clare.

"Yeah, Yeah. We've heard these kinds of things before," answers Trewella.

Morwen Penrose speaks next, "We want to make the UK a hostile environment for money laundering by targeting individuals to secure their prosecution and conviction and disrupting their techniques and recovering and confiscating assets. If Reverend Richards is a politically exposed person or corrupt elite we can use the Criminal Finances Act or an Unexplained Wealth Order to recover criminal assets.

"But," says Trewella, "But - we need hard evidence, not hearsay."

"That's where we can help," says Clare, "Finance is increasingly global, with money and assets moving quickly between jurisdictions, products and services. We can help you by showing traceable money flows which run through Clyst Richards."

"But we'll need your help," adds Bigsy.

"We've created a scheme, " says Clare, "to lure Leonard Richards."

"Sounds like entrapment to me," answers Trewella.

"Not strictly," says Clare, " We checked. The act of entrapment does not take away the intent to commit a guilty act from the accused.

In this sense, the entrapment has served its

purpose, as it observed a prohibited act, led to the arrest of the guilty party, and supposedly did not manipulate the guilty intent, only the circumstances of the guilty act.

Trewella answers, "Yes, although it can be used as mitigation in sentencing if the police or other government agents lure someone into committing a crime and then try to prosecute them for doing so.

This would be considered an abuse of court process and the judge could order a stay of the proceedings."

"It sounds as if you have been there?" asks Bigsy.

"In a manner of speaking," says Trewella, "But that's for another day."

Clare continues, " In this case, if you identify and arrest money launderers, you are able to disrupt further criminal activity, as well as making the UK a tough environment for those who seek to use it to launder criminal finances."

She adds, "And it's such a strange scheme, too. The Reverend is bringing a handful of migrants into the UK and then helping them get jobs. There are strings attached, and he is using these exploited people to help gather intelligence for another of his schemes."

Bigsy adds, "We don't believe Leonard Richards

is a kingpin in this. We think he is a convenient front."

"We want you to help us build a picture around one of our operatives. Her name is Li Mei. Chinese, rich and well-connected. She lives in Exeter."

Clare adds, "We'd like you to visit Reverend Richards and to ask him under advisement about Li Mei. Say that she is a member of his congregation, but that you have received information from the UK Financial Intelligence Unit of a Suspicious Activity Report. Richards will certainly know that a SAR is a critical intelligence resource for tackling money laundering, terrorism, serious and organised crime, corruption, and fraud. You can also tell the police that Li Mei goes under two identities...The other one is Cathy Kwan."

"You are baiting the line?" says Trewella.

"Yes, exactly," answers Clare, "Trying to catch the big fish."

Conference Call

The next day we are back in the hotel. We decide to use Clare's ultra-large room for a conference call with Christina. Clare has the Junior Suite, which offers a separate room for the call from the comfort of a sofa and a couple of chairs. Bigsy has rigged it up so that we can call Christina on an iPhone yet play the picture back on the big screen TV.

The ring tone sounds as if we are under water. Then, splosh, Christina answers. She looks happy and I think there's someone else in her room, but off camera.

"Hey," she says and blows us all a kiss, " I told Chuck we'd be meeting tonight and he said he'd like to tag along - we've been reminiscing about previous adventures!"

Chuck now moves into view and waves, "Hey, tell me to go away if you want to keep it small," he says.

"No, this is great," answers Clare for all of us.

"Oh - is that your room?" asks Christina, "You've done all right at that hotel!"

We smile but none of us ventures that only Clare got the ultra large room. A perk of making the booking, I'm guessing.

"So, what do we know now, and how will we take this forward?" asks Chuck.

"We've found out a few more things," says Clare, "First, our vicar is a front for the intel gathering. Bring in well-educated economic migrants, train them in the ways of the British and deploy them to gather information. Two sources, one for straightforward rubbish sifting and the other by the art of listening."

Christina agrees, "Exactly, it's what I've found too. The intel from the office cleaners is the best. The R&D people around Nine Elms are researching some kind of weather management device for Brant. It ties in with what they have found in Exeter. My guess is it is because the prior device ended in failure. The Brant RightMind project for hive military mobilisation was delayed after its AI systems went rogue. They are still working on it but moved it from Geneva to somewhere in north Norway."

Bigsy adds, "Brant have found ways to tame the

internet. We're back in a world of information highways, which feed into bottlenecks that the United States has unwittingly turned into Brant choke points. It allows surveillance and control of everyday commerce and interaction across the globe.

"It's very clever," says Chuck, "Brant are the mechanism being used by the United States. They support the networks and much of the processing."

Bigsy nods, "These networks carry the traffic of the global economy, supporting financial services and production systems. Brant has placed itself at the crossroads. In 1989, we saw the triumph of one world order over another, as the political and economic confrontation of the Cold War gave way to world-spanning networks. The Internet, global finance, and supply chains proliferated as business took advantage of new economic freedoms. "

Chuck interrupts, "Yes, after the 9/11 attacks, when the U.S. government was at its most vulnerable, Brant stumbled onto the political power hidden amid the plumbing of this new global economy. It is almost deliberate."

Bigsy nods again, "At first, the US sought to use these systems to target the 'bad guys.' Brant was very accommodating. Focused on the immediate threat of terrorists and rogue states, the agencies and bureaucracies involved didn't anticipate how the powers they were wielding would transform America's relationship with allies such as Europe, competitors like China, and the global business community. But Brant did."

Chuck smiles, "Nor did officials understand how tempting it would be to use network capabilities not just to subdue villains but to subjugate friends that had largely accepted interdependence as a source of market efficiencies."

Clare asks, "So was Washington, enabled by Brant, slowly but surely turned thriving economic networks into tools of domination? If so, the United States sleepwalked its way into a new struggle for empire, breaking bad without ever quite realising it!"

"Undoubtedly!" said Christina, "The coming disputes between empires can be turned to different purposes, closing down tax havens, or helping build the structures to fight climate change. But what can't be done is to map plausible escape routes from the underground empire. It's easy to descend into it but not so easy to get out."

"Hotel California, and with the right passcodes there are a multitude of secret passages to explore." says Bigsy.

Christina nods, "Some think that the answer is

simple: empire and global networks were different phases of a vast and complex plot, which has slowly unfolded over decades. Vladimir Putin claimed that the Internet is a CIA project designed to empower America by undermining Russia and other autocratic states.

Chuck adds, "Yes, and Putin seems to believe the Cold War never finished: it just evolved from power games in the shadow of nuclear confrontation to semi-clandestine information war, conducted via networks that were purposely built to be weaponised against America's adversaries."

"That's where things get really dark," says Christina, "The US thinks that Brant is subservient, but in practise they are a superpower."

Bigsy says, "Yes, those who built this new world claimed that they had put an end to old-style geopolitical manoeuvring between states. Instead of an old world divided by a wall we have a new one bound together by a web."

Chuck nods, "Yes and Brant must know exactly what they are doing, getting control of all the elements."

"Literally," adds Christina, "If they are able to control the climate too."

Chuck smiles ruefully, "Intimidate. Manipulate

the supply chains, control the finance, destroy crops if they are inconvenient. And hold back a big threat."

"Speak softly and carry a big stick," says Clare.

We all nod.

Christina adds, "Think about it. Governments would no longer control financial flows. Instead, financial flows would control governments, as politicians cowered in the face of changes to sovereign credit ratings. We learned in Arkhangelsk that no one would want to go to war in a world of globalised supply chains, since by attacking your neighbour, you would just be attacking your own economy. Think of the Ukrainian grain harvests demolished by the Russian war. Who gains? China. Even Putin failed to see that. He was intent on attacking Europe's bread basket and stepping away from the U.N. Grain Initiative. Brant's new world view is an emporium, a thriving marketplace where the very notion of empire is irrelevant despite using the moves of an empire to create the new structures.".

She pauses but then continues, "I consider the truth is more interesting and complicated than Putin's world of conspiracies. If the Cold War hadn't ended, the great era of global network building would never have begun. A world that was divided into mutually distrustful power blocs would never have allowed networks to entangle their economies together. Furthermore, it wasn't the United States government that built the networks. Following the collective wisdom of the day, officials believed that their job was to get out of the way of private enterprise, which was overwhelmingly U.S.-based or U.S.-focused. Step in, Brant."

Christina looks down the camera and I can sense that she is trying to figure out what we are thinking.

She softly adds, "These network builders were businesses and business consortiums, pursuing profit and efficiency rather than conquest. Conquest is an unintended consequence. Those who had political aspirations more often wanted to undermine empire rather than to maintain it, hoping that they were building a networked world in which people and private organisations would be able to make their own connections, regardless of whether their governments wanted to."

I see Bigsy and Clare nodding agreement.

Now it's Bigsy's turn, "This 'world without empire' seems remarkably familiar. Without any need for a grand plan, the map reflects and reinforces the Cold War victory of the United States. The networks that connect the world together don't just follow the contours of past economic and political power relations. These networks froze a moment in time, the brief period when the United States was at the apex of its power and at the centre of everything, so that it lasted for decades. "

He pauses, then says, "Take the undersea and underground cables that tied the world's communications system together. Most global Internet bandwidth passes through the United States. Even the global messaging system that allowed banks to talk with each other was based in Belgium—but its board was dominated by U.S. banks, and it was hostage to its data centre in Northern Virginia. International banks carried out international transactions in U.S. dollars, exposing them to the 'dollar clearing system,' a set of complex financial arrangements controlled by U.S. regulators. Even as the production of complex semiconductors moved from the United States to Asia, American companies kept key aspects of semiconductor design and intellectual property at home."

Chuck comments, "The pipes and plumbing of globalisation didn't just carry power to the centre. They also made it more vulnerable to attacks, as the United States found out on September 11, 2001. Decentralised communications systems made it much easier for terrorists to communicate, while an open global financial system allowed them to send money and resources across borders unimpeded."

He adds, "But so long as the United States had the will to change things, the means were close at hand. Key global networks were centred on the United States, allowing U.S. authorities in the NSA, the Department of the Treasury, and elsewhere to turn the broader network to their own purposes."

Christina adds, "The global economy relied on the pre-constructed tunnels and conduits that the United States could move into and adapt, nearly as easily as if they had been custom designed by a military engineer for that purpose. By seizing control of key intersections, the U.S. government could secretly listen to what adversaries were saying to each other or freeze them out of the global financial system."

I was thinking about the hidden power in such things, of which most are blissfully unaware.

Chuck says, "At the beginning, the U.S. government seized this opportunistically sporadically. U.S. officials saw themselves as responding to an immediate, urgent threat rather than self-consciously building the foundations of a new kind of power. When the United States deployed this power, it targeted terrorist organisations like Al-Qaeda and belligerent states with few friends, like North Korea. Some of what the United States did was controversial, but the disagreements mostly centred on sweeping interpretations of presidential power."

"China was quick to emulate this," says Christina, "Russia wanted to but came up with other more blunt instrument hacks instead."

Bigsy, "Yet governments, too, can follow paths without anticipating where they lead. As departments and agencies developed new tools, they kept on finding new uses for them. Whenever a new use was discovered, it created a possible precedent for others. When bureaucrats got a taste of power, they liked it. America's control of global communication networks allowed it to tap into the communications of allies as well as adversaries. "

Chuck smiles, "You are right Bigsy. Before the Internet, surveillance was difficult and expensive, meaning that it was usually reserved for 'high-value targets': terrorists, senior foreign officials, and other people whose communications were strategically valuable. After September 11, U.S. surveillance agencies had free rein and massive resources, which they used to turn global telecommunications networks into a distributed surveillance system. They literally built a system that allowed them to record every single phone call in an entire country and store the data for up to a month, so that they could later "rewind" individual conversations that they suspected might be interesting."

Clare smiles, "After the fact - these monstrous audit trails only provide retroactive intelligence. After something has happened, you can trace back to find out how it occurred. Useful for a blame game, but not so useful for prediction."

Chuck agrees, "Yes, it's amazing that we all got away with it. A huge investment programme but really it wasn't all that useful, although it helped generate huge incomes for some contractors."

"Including Brant?" asks Clare.

"Oh yes and then some," smiles Chuck, "In this new world, the problem wasn't gathering information. It was storing the massive amounts of data that were collected and sifting them for valuable nuggets. When the U.S. government started taking full advantage of America's position in global networks, its surveillance state was transformed."

Christina adds, "Beyond the data was the financial coercion. The U.S. Department of the Treasury had started to aggressively investigate its options for gathering data from the world, so that it could detect future attacks. It quickly identified the SWIFT (Society for Worldwide Interbank Financial Telecommunication) messaging system—which plays a core role in global financial transfers—as a crucial source of information and demanded access to SWIFT's information under pain of criminal subpoenas.

We studied this at Arkhangelsk. One of our tasks was to see how we could run interference."

Chuck adds, "Treasury also began to develop a new kind of sanction, which used its control of 'dollar clearing' to force international banks to implement U.S. policy outside its borders. Control of SWIFT and dollar clearing were combined to cut Iran out of the world's financial system, forcing it to the negotiating table to discuss its nuclear weapons program.

That's real economic leverage," says Clare, "Far more than a diplomat standing on a jetway."

Chuck continues. "The U.S. officials who planned these steps often thought of them as once-off emergency measures. Not for long. Instead, they became the precedent for a more general transformation of U.S. financial power. Slowly, and without ever really thinking through what it was doing, the United States transformed the subterranean networks that tied the world's economy together into an underground empire, where it could listen in on the world's conversations and isolate its enemies from the world economy. There was a big policy slide. Once-radical proposals became commonplace tools of policy. The United States was no longer just the world's remaining superpower. It was a state with superpowers. Like a spider at the heart of a global web, it could detect the subtle drum beats of what enemies and friends were saying to each other from thousands of miles away. And when it thought it necessary, it could tightly wrap an adversary's economy in smothering strands stronger than steel."

Clare adds, "But with great power comes great responsibility. Officials began to worry about what they had wrought. Brant established itself as a fully embedded player. The Snowden revelations, which detailed secret U.S. surveillance efforts had not only left the American intelligence community on the back foot but threatened the political arrangements underlying the Internet.

Chuck mutters, "So Christina's original thoughts seem to be right. There's a three-layer plan being worked out by Brant. It's got access to the communications infrastructure, then to the banking systems and finally to above the earth climate management. Brant is almost godlike."

Delicate

"Look," says Penrose, "This is a delicate situation: a well-known accountancy firm moved £1bn for Dmitri Sagadeyev Leonid (Lyonya) Fyodorovich the Russian tycoon on the very day he was put under sanctions. Some files were leaked and raised questions over deal timings. The disclosure raises serious questions about the role played by the accountants in a potential sanctions breach."

"Kind of like some of those other high-profile leaks, " says Bigsy.

Penrose continues, "Yes, although less well publicised. Details of the blue-chip accountant's work for the Kremlin-connected tycoon emerged when a cache of 3.6m offshore records were leaked to the Affiliation of Investigative Journalists (AIJ) which shared access with the Sentinel and other media partners."

Bigsy shakes his head, "No, I've not heard of this

one, unless it has a name like 'The Corsica Papers, or something?"

Penrose continues, "They gave this one a code word: 'Church'. It's because it could implicate a member of the local clergy. The data totals 1.3 terabytes of confidential financial files, amounting to more than 3.6m documents and other records. They originate from six offshore service providers that set up, manage and list shell companies and trusts in Corsica – as well as a company that sells access to Cypriot company data."

"I assume our colleague Grace Fielding knows about this. If access to the records from the leak was shared by the AIJ, then I'd expect the Organised Crime and Corruption Reporting Project to be involved," says Bigsy.

Penrose looks at Bigsy, "We researched this further. Corsica, an EU member state, has long served as an important offshore financial centre for wealthy Russians who have favoured the Mediterranean island as a gateway to move their fortunes out of their home country and into Europe. Clients of the companies in the leak include Russian oligarchs who are now under sanctions."

Clare looks puzzled, "But holding assets in offshore havens such as Corsica, sometimes via trusts, is not in or of itself illegal, and there are legitimate reasons why some people do it."

Penrose nods, "You are correct. There are some extremely well-known politicians involved. The files contain emails in which the accounting staff discuss attempting to transfer about a third of the shares in an extremely well-known European company to Alina Petrovna, the life partner of the business tycoon Adam Antonovich. The move shines a light on the services that blue-chip advisers performed for wealthy Russian clients, amid a debate about the timings of when EU sanctions become fully active."

Bigsy looks excited, "We know that Alina tricked her supposed boss Colonel General Kovarin. Remember, he was a nasty piece of work in any case using fléchettes fired from Anti-tank weapons against his enemies."

"Barbarous weapons," says Trewella, unaware of her accidental pun, "Yet, since the invasion of Ukraine, western governments have imposed the largest ever package of sanctions against Russia and its business elite, and attention is now turning to ensuring those restrictions are enforced."

He continues, " Of course, the accountancy firm said it was unaware of any criminal investigation. In response to information in the leaked files, a spokesperson for the accounting firm gave a line in PR bullshit."

Penrose nods, "We discovered that Corsica and Cyprus have both acted as gateway for Russian fortunes into Europe. Our analysis of the files suggests that 31 Corsican clients were named on sanctions lists last year by the US, the UK, the EU, or Ukraine after the 2022 invasion.

Then she says, "The accountant's headquarters are locally owned and operate under collective standards in return for using the accounting group's brand. On the day Russia invaded, Alina Petrovna was one of the 36 business leaders who met Vladimir Putin at the Kremlin, according to the EU."

I can't help thinking how much their savvy has improved since the earlier case.

Trewella adds, "Three days after the Ukrainian invasion, on Sunday 27 February, Europe's foreign ministers gathered by video conference to agree a fresh round of sanctions. On the same day, the EU's most senior diplomat said the latest sanctions were imminent, that they would be targeted at oligarchs, and were likely to be active before the start of business the next day."

I pause to consider. This has moved on from a dodgy vicar importing migrants for espionage to something altogether more global. I can see how Leonard Richards is considered as a front man.

I'd originally thought his actions were like a

'long firm fraud'. That he was using his charity created for fraudulent purposes. The basic operation is to run the so-called charity legitimately. Once sufficiently well-established, the perpetrators begin their mischief. In a conventional long firm fraud, it would be to decamp with goods and profits from previous sales. This time it's a whole lot more subtle with leverage being applied to the migrant workers. And not forgetting these procedures need a certain amount of money to set up, often the proceeds from previous crime.

The Mafia used to be good at this kind of thing. Conventional long firm frauds are significantly less common now because of computerised audit trails. But the charity angle provides a new mechanism. One thing was becoming clear. Richards was in it up to his dog collar.

Kingfisher

Despite the stress, there are times back at the hotel for reflection. My huge plate glass window looks out onto a woodland path, which I guess is there because of power lines. There's a stream too, and I've seen dog walkers out along the route. Maybe occasional cyclists too, but its bumpiness makes it heavier going.

One day, I noticed a small bird shoot skyward, and I released by its flash of blue that it was a kingfisher. It had been in reeds in an area that was once a small pond, where the stream's water gathered. Then I saw it drop again onto one reed and almost vanish from view. I decided it must be hunting, an eternal optimist looking for small fish in the pond.

Then I saw something clever. A raggle-taggle scattering of starlings was making their way along the stream. And as they flew past the kingfisher, it launched itself into the middle of them. Hiding in plain sight.

The Setup

The warning to Icarus, as he stretched out his wings for the first time seemed straightforward enough:: "Don't fly too near the sun, nor the sea. One will melt the wax, and the other weigh down the feathers. Keep to the middle course."

That's what we needed for our plan with Li Mei. She had been approached by Zoe now and was completely willing to be involved in our plot. All she needed was confidence, which she seemed to possess with swagger.

Most of the time, confidence carries a self-correcting balance. Some days to wake up with head in the clouds and to have to remind ourselves to stay grounded. Other days, it's as if we are just barely slogging through, hoping something can lift spirits. But it's not always that simple. Sometimes we all do not know what to think, feeling somehow better than everybody but not good enough for anybody. This is actually when we are at our most precarious, feeling overdue for a correction.

It was that kind of day explaining what we'd devised for Li Mei.

At any moment we expected something to throw us off-balance, as we fly into spiralling self-doubt, with it picking apart our wings, as we try to figure out if our feathers are still attached.

"I can do this," says Li Mei, "I can be the big shot - I've watched my stepfather do it enough times...seen him trample over lesser folk. I need to tell them I have vast money flows, which I need them to clean. I can imply that it's linked with my stepfather's business - Quanban. If they ask me where it is from, I will tell them to mind their own business.

She looks around, "Chuck, Christina you'll be there to help me, but I'd like to take Zoe into this as well. She can help me revise the part and will then know my entire back-story."

"I'll be your assistant," says Zoe, "It's one up from when I was a chambermaid at Magister Grange."

They hug.

"Great, says Li Mei, "That's settled then."

You think over your life and realise how much of it is mythology. The stories you tell yourself. How many half-hearted compliments have you taken to heart, how many of your friendships hold together by little more than circumstance?

This is one of those moments. A big, yet unreliable, one. The forging together of assets - sassy assets, which cause us to overlook just one small thing.

You may love your partner but doubt how well that comes across. You may love your job but question if it's worth all the time it has cost you, knowing how easily your role could be refilled, your legacy tossed in a box. You wonder if you're really any good at it or have been ignoring warning signs that it is time to try something else.

This is that something. It's what makes us happy. Finding the line between self-actualisation and self-indulgence? And guarding that line. Protecting it. Will this make a difference? Then again, what difference could we realistically hope to make?

Perhaps we tell ourselves it doesn't matter as long as we do something- but wouldn't that only prove we were doing it just for ourselves, not for some greater cause? So where does that leave us?

You begin to wonder if you've spent your entire

life buoyed by airy delusions, coasting along on unearned confidence. But if it's possible to carry on that way indefinitely and not even notice, does it even matter whether any of it is real?

Maybe our self-mythology does not differ from any other mythology? It's a story that changes in the telling, evolving over time. Whatever resonates will stay, and what doesn't will fall away. To pick away at the literal truth is to miss the point, miss the joy of it. So, build your myth. Try to tell a good story about yourself that captures something true, whether the facts agree.

Keep to the middle course. Steal bits of wax and feathers discarded by other, better fliers. Let the sun rise and fall. Let the waves pound themselves to mist, again and again. Our task is not to be flawless.

Our task is to fly.

Details

"Le bon Dieu est dans le détail"
(literally "the good God is in the detail")
Gustave Flaubert (1821–1880)

"Der liebe Gott steckt im detail"
Aby Warburg (1866–1929)

"God is in the details"
Ludwig Mies van der Rohe (1886-1969)

"The devil and the angels are in the details."
US House Speaker Nancy Pelosi (2020)

Rehearsal

We rehearse the story for Reverend Richards. Li Mei is the front for a conglomerate based in Ashburn, Virginia. Maybe she is implausibly young, but that was the allure of the plan. A fresh-faced Chinese student fronting up an organised crime supergroup. We loosely based her story on her stepfather Ren Mei and his Quanban company.

Li Mei represents an enterprise called Kanbashi (香し). Kanbashi is Japanese for 'sweet smelling and of good reputation'. Clever to take the Brant-based Quanban and flip its name into the independent Kanbashi, They even sound very similar.

Richards would realise (as would his masters) that Li Mei must be the face of something undisclosed yet criminal. Bigsy had soon rigged up an internet presence for the new organisation, partly by 'borrowing' from a few other corporates. Kanbashi of Tokyo fictitiously ran large data centres and a logistics empire.

And now Li Mei's organisation had cashflow challenges, creating more free cash than was healthy and it wanted to put this cash away in some kind of structured facility.

It could seem implausible, but Li Mei had the right moves. It was tempting for Brant, because they could clandestinely absorb Kanbashi in the same way as Quanban. China and now Japan.

Why was Li Mei in Exeter? A perfect cover story. Not living flashily on superyachts and Caribbean islands. She was the front for Kanbashi yet still at university. Li Mei wanted to break from her father's firm, owned as it was by Brant. By setting up the connection to an independent company, she could make the jump. She had amassed a fortune of her own, ironically using Quanban's own legal department and could now become entirely self-sufficient.

And the story was partly about a boy. She had fallen in love with her boyfriend Daniel Wendling and wanted to get clear from the organisation which was dominating both their lives. Therefore, this was a one-time deal after which she would disappear.

"It sounds too good to be true," says Christina.

"It does," says Li Mei, "Like some kind of Young Adult Tik-Tok romance."

"Pressure, it needs pressure," says Chuck.

"I'm being hunted by debtors," says Li Mei, "They want an increased cut. It's why I'm getting out."

"Why Exeter?" says Christina.

"It's because I've been working towards the meeting with Leonard Richards for a very long time," answers Li Mei, "I've researched him and know about his business,"

"That makes you a threat," says Christina.

"Ah, but I only know about this one possible deal," answers Li Mei, "So my research hasn't been that thorough,"

"Good," says Christina, " You are finding a middle way."

"Between the sea and the sun," replies Li Mei.
I think I've underestimated her.

Meeting Richards

I'll skim over the messy part where we try to set up the meeting with Leonard Richards. It was in several parts. Meet him at his church. Tell the story. Give him a chance to research it and no doubt tell his bosses. Flash some initial cash - thanks to Amanda.

Then, finally, a meeting in Exeter. It was to be in the Assembly Room at the Clyst Richards facility. Dramatically, Li Mei arranged to fly in by helicopter. She even asked Christina to pilot her craft - a Kamov 62.

"It's the same as the fighter version, but has been made prettier and luxurious," says Christina, "No missile launchers either."

"What's the air spoiler for on the tail?" I ask.

"Trim," says Christina, "They have a lot of imported parts, so different models look surprisingly different."

"Weren't they a commercial flop?" asks Chuck.

Christina replies with a twinkle, “Yes, after one part failure, Bulgaria collared the second-hand market and resprayed and refitted them as KA-62s. But for people who know, they are rare collectors' items. Like arriving in an old luxurious Bugatti car."

Now we are circling the H Zone at the Richards' property. Christina is flying the helicopter with Chuck as a co-pilot.

Chuck smiles, "You are doing all the work, Christina."

She smiles back, "If it was next week we'd have the Torbay air show to contend with. They fly planes all over this area. Everything from Lancaster bombers to Eurofighters. Then, I promise, you'd be busy!""

Chuck smiles, "Those Eurofighters are something else. The latest ones are even intelligent."

"I've tried them, although their combat helmets are powered by Brant RightMind technology. It's supposed to be a hive mind AI concept. But it's too slow."

Also on board are Zoe, me, and Li Mei. I'm wearing a pseudo military outfit which makes me look like a Mall cop. My entire face is covered in a big black scarf and dark glasses. I don't even recognise myself. Chuck wears his outfit so much better and genuinely looks the part. Hard man mercenary.

Christina is in leather flying garb and Li Mi and Zoe Demelza are in glamorous warm civilian clothing. Li Mei is in a black, soft coat, prune coloured trousers, merino wool turtleneck and impractically high shoes. She sexily looks the part of the boss. Zoe has an outsized green parka, with no hood, a white tee, back jeans, and military boots. She looks badass.

"Distraction is key," says Christina, "Keep them wondering."

We land. A big, featureless, shed-sized SUV pulls up and we are whisked to the Assembly Room.

Penelope is there to greet us. "I know you," she says to me, "You came to that meeting?"

I nod conspiratorially.

"Ah, I see," she says and smiles enigmatically. She gestures to a large man standing outside our meeting room. "Watch this one," she says playfully.

Then I see her. Stéphane Gérard: Bettina Kübler's friend and someone who I sat opposite at Jago's Magister Grange dinner party. I remember she worked in weather systems and Kübler worked in eDefence.

"Jake - It's not what you might think," she says, pointedly gesturing to a partition blocking the corner of the room. I realise Richards must have suspected us of something for a considerable time.
Then Leonard Richards arrives, suited but with a dog collar sign of priesthood.

He smiles, "I knew it. That you were not what you seemed. We had you down as an advanced party. You and that Bigsy...Is he here?"

"He's back in our hotel actually," I say. I'm slightly troubled that we were identified so quickly and now I'm wondering if our soufflé is about to collapse.

But no, money, it seems, always talks.

"That was a most generous initial donation," says Penelope, to Li Mei.
Li Mei smiles, "Think of it as a sign of intent...We want to move a considerably larger sum to a safe haven."

Li Mei is good, really good at being bad.

How much?" asks Leonard.

"Say four million US," answers Li Mei, "Once a

month to begin with, then once a week when we can see how everything is working out."

"That's a very large sum," says Leonard, "It will take a little while to set up."

"I'll want it spread around, undetectably," says Li Mei. I can see she has learnt some tricks from her father. Mainly 'cut to the chase.'

"We can do that, " answers Leonard.

Another woman steps forward from behind the tall, grey, material office divider that Stéphane Gérard had indicated. I'm amazed to see it is Alina Petrovna. She doesn't appear to recognise me. I notice Christina shift her stance, quietly covering the room.

"I'm here for Brant," says Petrovna, "we assist Reverend Richards. Sponsor him in a manner of speaking."

"Why Brant?" I ask.

"We have certain global interests, intentions even" she answers.

I get it, she is talking about world domination. A corporation, ostensibly American, but with deep Russian interests. A Putin plan. I remember that Petrovna is ruthless having taken out her predecessor. Suitable caution required.

"We'll need some collateral whilst we run the first transaction," she says.

I notice no introductions. She's the boss, alright.

"That's people, by the way, not money. Your parents, Li Mei. I think you are still fond of them?"

Li Mei shifts uneasily. I remember she is an actress too. But family members. Alina is taking it too far.

"Sure," Li Mei says, "But it's reciprocal, you realise? There are several ways that this could go sideways."

Wow, she plays hard ball. Now Alina looks mildly surprised.

Li Mei smiles, "But look, we all want this to work, don't we? Even Reverend Richards would like to get his 5%."

"Five percent for nothing," replies Petrovna, "Nice work if you can get it."

I sense she has used up her song title collection of phrases by now.

Then she says "Quarter Million Dollars"

Another song title. I'm thinking - '50 rubber

bands'.

Leonard looks confused but Penelope nods. They'll make a tidy $250,000 from every transaction. Four months to a million dollars. And it's clean, I'm guessing. Let the good times roll. Oops, now I'm doing it.

I hear a gentle click, then another couple. Chuck holds up his hands. "Not me, " he declares.

"It's okay, but we had to be sure," Alina rolls back a screen. There's an RPK-16 mounted on a combat tripod behind it. I know the shells would simply rip through the room divider as if it was transparent. The gunner is wearing ear protectors. The weapon could stop a small tank.

"Li Mei smiles, "Our weapons are less obvious but just as effective," I know she is bluffing but it sure sounds real.

"Right. We will deliver a laptop here tomorrow, with a lawyer to confirm arrangements. It has the fund instructions on it. Get it right. The laptop self-destructs after it has executed the transfer."

We prepare to leave. It has been a short meeting. The fastest transfer of funds I've ever seen negotiated.

In. Deep.

We all wait until Christina is flying our craft along the River Exe, clear of Clyst Richards.

Zoe asks, "Could they shoot us down?"

"But why? They have just got everything they wanted. We have delightfully fallen into their laps." answers Bigsy.

I notice Christina, Zoe and Li Mei all do involuntary wriggles.

"What about Stéphane Gérard?" I ask, "Why was she there?"

"I suspect she was a kind of hostage," answers Christina, "however unwitting. They had her there and visible to ensure we would all behave. Of course, she is a witness now, getting in rather deep."

"Yes, they are implicating her, even if she was an unwitting bystander, and by connection her partner Bettina Kübler," answers Christina, " That's classy leverage."

"That gun was a Spetznaz weapon," says Chuck. Christina nods in agreement, "Alina has friends in high places,"

"Low places," says Zoe, "They could have murdered us all in that hall."

"It was posturing," says Chuck, "Saying don't mess with us. Li Mei, you were sensational. Not a waver!"

"To be honest I quite enjoyed it; I'm not so sure I would if I'd realised there was a machine gun behind that barrier. They must really want this thing to work."

"Yes, and they could hardly achieve that by killing us all. Now we need to bring them the laptop with some of Amanda's funds. She will be pleased we have limited this first payment to $4 million!"

"How much is the helicopter?" asks Chuck, looking at Christina.

"It's okay, my father paid for it. Like I said, we are really well - off, but I seldom get any chance to express it," answers Li Mei.

"The price of a small car, just for today, with me as a certified pilot," answers Christina.

"Sheesh," says Chuck, "Buckle in and enjoy it! I guess we'll use a motor cycle courier to deliver the laptop?"

"And we'll need a lawyer to visit as well to 'finalise arrangements'," says Li Mei.

"Scrub the motorcycle, you'll need a black limo," says Chuck smiling.

"Yes we can hire something expensive from one of the firms in Exeter," answers Zoe.

"But the lawyer...who can we trust?" asks Chuck.

"What about Grace?" asks Christina, "She scrubs up well and looks professional when suited and booted."

"But she is not field," says Chuck.

"But this is entirely safe, and she is a smart cookie," answers Christina, "Cheltenham to Exeter? Heck, we could use the limo firm to transport her in comfort!"

We smile conspiratorially, secretly thinking of Amanda's reaction to the request.

Limo

A big Mercedes sedan, the same kind than Bigsy owns, but tricked out in mirror finish black coach livery and with a longer wheelbase. Televisions in the back (notice its plural).

Grace will have the journey of her lifetime coming down to Exeter. We've arranged for her to visit us at the hotel too, both before and after her visit to Clyst Richards.

And she gets a new name for the visit. Alexandra Finch. Alex, of course. Amanda didn't blow a gasket that we wanted to use Grace for this part and confided that it was good for Grace's development to get some field work.

Grace was excited by the whole thing, which we promised her was entirely safe. Li Mei bribed the driver to let Bigsy take the wheel and the original driver had a free day in Cheltenham.

So many moving parts...

They arrive at the hotel. Bigsy has explained everything to Grace/Alex, and they even stopped at the A303 farm shop services in Somerset on the way down. Bigsy now has a supply of very large sausage rolls.

Grace speaks, "So this is a simple situation. I ask them to digitally sign for the fund transfer and refer off to separate terms and conditions."

"That's how my father does this kind of thing. Frankly the lawyers are usually more hidden that we are making them, it's not a Mafia movie," says Li Mei.

"But they do carry guns," mumbles Chuck, "Sorry Alex, but nothing will go wrong, and anyway Christina is riding 'shotgun' for you. They'll expect that, but it won't present a problem.

Christina smiles at Grace. I can see Christina's roving eve picking out the detail from what must have been Grace's most expensive business suit.

Grace smiles, "Li Mei was most generous, but I decided to get this pre-owned piece."

It's a Chanel black skirt suit with offset floral gold buttons which accentuate Grace's figure. The collar is high around the neck. Delightful and the small Balmain orange-brown bag is a lovely flourish.

"It still cost more than a month's apartment rental," says Grace, "But you'd never know it was pre-owned. I think it can only have been worn once. And this bag cost even more than the suit."

Christina coos in a way that I've not heard before.

"The laptop doesn't fit," says Bigsy, "But it's okay - I found a manilla envelope and have put the laptop inside. He shows it to us with a mild flourish, "It's fully charged."

So now it's 'game on', although we won't know how it goes until they return to us at the hotel.

Something else I haven't told you

"There is one other thing," says Grace, "We found out what else Brant were looking for."

"Let me guess," says Chuck, "Weather Management?"

"You are good," says Grace, "But in a very specialised form. They want to use stealth to manipulate the weather."

"Like we found in those discarded drawings," says Christina.

"It's like a multi-part thing," Says Grace, "They are using Ground Effect Vehicles to set targeting. The source weapon is in geostationary orbit. At 35,786 kilometres orbiting the equator."

"I see, it moves at the same rate as the earth rotates, " says Clare.

"Exactly," says Grace. "It is always over the same point." A bit like Grace really, I muse, always 'on point'.

"I can see this," says Chuck, "But what about the targeting? That's where the GEV comes in, I guess?"

"Right, again," says Grace. "They manoeuvre a fast, slippery target sled (that's the Ground Effect Vehicle) to exactly where they want to target the weapon. Brant makes the GEVs. No surprises there. Then, using an orbiting three-beam Trigax rail gun (also made by Brant) they can concentrate a high intensity beam to that exact spot. One of the beams is deeply supercooled quasi stationary plasma. I know, it sounds like Ghostbusters, but it's a real thing! Then, a blend of all three beams can produce a mixture of mayhem, and it's that combination that can disrupt climate patterns."

"Wow, it's far more impressive than dropping silver iodide out of a B52," says Chuck.

"And infinitely less detectable," says Grace, "For example, a GEV sled can be manoeuvred to near a targeting area by road or sea, then released and travel the last part undetected. The sleds are about the size of a small car, only flatter."

"It's all illegal nowadays," says Chuck, "We were shut down and told not to use weather weapons any more.

"Kinda true," says Grace, "But America created Senate Bill 1807 and House Bill 3445, back in July 2007, to establish a Weather Mitigation Advisory and Research Board to fund weather modification research. It's still a technology in play."

"I see, but they cleared out all the people (like me) who had previous involvement, so the Brant could get money to invent it all over again!"

We all look involuntarily towards the sky.

'Rain down on me, ' as the OK Computer song goes.

PART THREE

Natural Order

Natural order encompasses the natural relations of beings to one another in the absence of law, which natural law attempts to reinforce.

In contrast, divine law seeks authority from God, and positive law seeks authority from government.

Cf. Way of Man vs Way of Nature

Oh Me, Oh Life

Now Brant wants to interfere with nature.

But I remember we are guests here on Earth. Our life is not just a quest, or an opportunity, or a story to tell; it's also an experience, to be lived for its own sake. It doesn't have to mean anything other than what it is. A single moment can still stand on its own, as a fragment of existence.

Brant would rather have us doing something else. Brant wants control. After a minute or two, we feel our hand reaching for our phone or the car radio, eager to drown out thoughts with distractions. Perhaps there's a part that's instinctively wary of lingering too long in any one moment. Brant nurtures addiction and dependency. There is no time to think properly.

We can breathe this world in and hold on to it as long as we can, but we can't just stop there. We have to keep moving, digging around for some deeper meaning, hoping to find an escape hatch between one experience and the next. So, we never feel stuck inside one little moment, one little life. Fear Of Missing Out.

Brant wants us to be pre-occupied. To abandon critical thinking.

It's easy to forget that most of our memories happen in places that are still around, the walls are mostly unchanged, carrying on in our absence. But the world we knew, and the people we remember, have moved on.

It's almost impossible to imagine while we're still in it, experiencing the now. We know the crowds will soon be gone, the lights shut off, the music silenced. If we spend enough time in a place, it becomes infused with a certain meaning, with specific memories soaked deep into every corner. It's hard to imagine that it could ever mean anything else.

Brant doesn't want me to know I'm unique and surrounded by billions of other people, just as unique as me. Brant wants control. Domination.

Each of us is different, with some new angle on the world. Bigsy's or Chuck's or Christina's, even our late entrant Li Mei. So, what does it mean if the lives we're busy shaping all end up looking the same? Brant knows about this. It wants to control the spreadsheet, to be an overarching hand.

We all spread out, looking around for scraps of frontier, the edges, as we try to capture something special, something personal. But when we gather all our scattered snapshots side by side, the results are often uncannily similar. There's the same close-up of an eye, the same raindrops on a window, the same selfie in the side-view mirror. The airplane wingtip, the pair of bare legs stretched out on a beach chair. People photograph the same meals again and again. The same monuments pinched between fingers. The same waterfalls. Sunset after sunset.

Brant wants to substitute its own version of reality. Show everyone who Brant considers to be in charge. It's the same old, same old story. The story seeks comfort that we're not so different, that our perspectives so neatly align. If nothing else, it's a reminder that we all live in this same world with tarnished god-substitute corporations. Still, it makes you wonder. It makes us wonder how many of our snapshots could be easily replaced by a thousand identical others. Brant thinks it knows. Knows how to control.

Is there any value left in taking yet another photo of the moon, or the Taj Mahal, or the Eiffel Tower? Is a photograph just a kind of souvenir to prove we've been someplace, like a prefabricated piece of furniture we had assembled?

No, I think if we infuse it with originality, then it becomes a net contribution. A plus one.

It's alright if we tell the same jokes we've all heard before. That Chinese one about Stevie Wonder. It's alright if we keep remaking the same movies. Gone in Sixty Seconds becomes 10 minutes after the sequels. We can keep repeating the same phrases to each other as if we've never heard them before, and that's alright. Even when we look back to the earliest known work of art in existence, we'll find a handprint stencilled on the wall of a cave. Not one, but hundreds.

To be sure, you and I and billions of others will leave our mark on this world we've inherited, just like the billions who came before us. But if we find ourselves with nothing left to say, nothing new to add, idly tracing outlines left by others long ago - it would be as if we were never here at all. But no. Brant doesn't understand. We are all additive stardust.

This too, is not an original thought. Walt Whitman said, "The powerful play goes on, and you will contribute a verse." What else is there to say? When you get your cue, you say your line. Tender sadness, pensive melancholy, and leaves of grass.

But before that, Brant wants a piece of us.

Not if we get there first.

Highlight reel

I know this is sounding like a highlight reel. Like every moment has potential and there's something transcendent, hidden all around.

But we are seizing the day, holding it to carry along. The truth is, most of life is forgotten instantly, almost as it's happening. So, when something as intense as this situation comes along, it's worth savouring.

Seldom do we ever meet money launderers, gangster types with links to the Russian mafia. Let alone negotiate with them. A cadre of friends combining in an ultimate deception. Against evil - an evil empire, one might say.

Another day, another week, another year: such is the rhythm of ordinary time. Filled with long, featureless stretches, which we skip over to get to the good parts. The thousand acts of maintenance you have to do every day. The labour of keeping your body going, hauling it back and forth across the same stretch of road, no closer than you were the day before. You keep breathing in and out. Things fall apart; you clean up the mess. And it all washes away in the night, to be built up again in the morning. You keep throwing the week against the wall to see what sticks, hoping you'll remember something that happened today.

Anything.

These days will stay in our memory. We're taking on a mega-state, concealed Russian doll-like inside an American enterprise and with the cherry on top of a vicar to front everything.

And the mega-state is playing for keeps, with an underground strategy to capture the infrastructure that binds the world, then a control layer to run the money and politics and a super-structure to dictate the climactic terms.

We all know this is a singular moment, when we can finally say, "Eureka! I've found it!"

But the rest of life is happening anyway, whether or not we remember it.

Too good to be true

It was all going too well. Everything had fallen into place. Li Mei was believable; we had a great reference story about money to be washed and even had direct funding from the UK Secret Service.

What could possibly go wrong?

Everything.

Li Mei's stepfather became the weak link. Li Mei had changed her name to Cathy Kwan to distance herself from Ren Mei, the owner of a satellite communications company. Great plan whilst it lasted.

Dishy-Dishy? No, Dieshikeji! Ren Mei's company became Quánbān zu you, but because of their extraordinary technological prowess were later taken over by...you guessed it...Brant Technologie.

Why was I not surprised? I should have linked Brant and Quanban sooner.

Li Mei informed us, "Remember that my father Ren Mei was apprehended for breaking U.S. sanctions against Iran?" He did play it fairly fast and loose."

She adds, “A subsidiary of Ren Mei's company functioned as Quanban's Iran-based subsidiary. My stepfather was rescued in a plea bargain. A deferred prosecution agreement assisted by Brant meant he could walk free."

Li Mei can see we are all watching her intently "However, Brant pulled the strings, but it left Ren Mei with a debt of gratitude. It's when I became Cathy Kwan, left Paris, and came to Exeter to continue my robotics and AI study. Why two names? Li Mei for close friends, but Kathy Kwan was my kind of 'public' name - it's much easier for Brits to pronounce it correctly. You know something, even Li Mei is a reversed name because we Chinese usually put the ancestral surname first."

She looks at us intently, "My father has spotted the big spending on helicopter hire and expensive clothes and in the excitement I've forgotten to give him a reason. Because of Quanban, he's also been to Çlyst Richards a couple of times, so he knows about Brant having a base here in Exeter.

"He called me last night from Paris and asked whether everything was okay. I was caught off-guard and couldn't think up a story quickly enough, so I told him we were sightseeing along the river in the helicopter. My stepfather is an experienced negotiator and could easily spot my fib. He wanted to know why I was suddenly so interested in Clyst Richards."

I could feel our well-executed plan unravelling.

"It turns out my father also knows Alina Petrovna as a business acquaintance - I had no idea. She called him yesterday and asked him directly what his daughter was doing negotiating with Reverend Richards. Alina thought it was my stepfather up to his old tricks. He denied it, of course, but I sense the walls are closing in. Not only that, but Alina also said she would have to consider the Clyst Richards operation to be a weakness now."

"She warned my father to stay away from the area and to tell me to stay away also. Something was about to happen."

I decided it wouldn't be pretty to be on the wrong end of Alina's wrath.

Intense

We're all together in a huge, rented SUV. It's dark blue colour. Some kind of Mercedes monster truck driven by Bigsy. We've gone off road and can see the greenery from the edge of Clyst Richards sloping down to the river.

Additionally, we've notified Penrose and Trewella, and they have taken cover in a black police Land Rover, located further back along the same road as us.

This river flows out into the English Channel and then west toward the North Atlantic. Just across from the headland at Exmouth there are the famous train tracks of the Cornish Riviera Express, which runs through Dawlish and then on to Penzance at the very tip of Cornwall. Dawlish is well-known for storm waves which occasionally lash its shoreline, although it also has one of the most picturesque railways in the country. And on our side of the river, it remains sheltered and mild.

The first note is always the loudest.

Beethoven's Fifth: GGGF, played short-short-short LONG. Morse code V. Victory.

The conductor cracks their baton, strings slash and the symphony thunders.

So, with every new experience. This time it starts with a mammoth low-flying transport plane. Grey and marked with USAF insignia.

"It's a C-17 Globemaster!" calls Chuck, "They are big enough to carry the President's Marine One helicopter inside!"

"And the stretched limo!" adds Christina. "The US President doesn't know how to pack light!"

"I can feel the ground shaking," says Bigsy, "This one must be in the air show."

Then, suddenly in a puff, a tangle of smaller planes shimmer past, bright orange tails ablaze.

"Air dominance," says Chuck, "Eurofighters - Typhoons. The marines along at Lympstone must be beside themselves!"

Christina adds, "But one Mig-41 in that pack - see the twin tails and ultra-enormous engines."

"I have never seen a Mig-41!"says Chuck,

excitedly.

"Until today. It's hiding in plain sight. A kingfisher among the starlings," says Christina.

"Who needs the airshow," I say, "When we've got all of this on our doorstep."

"Riverbank," corrects Christina, "And that Mig is still top secret and one of the fastest planes on earth. No reason for it to be here in the Torbay Air Show!"

How quickly each feeling fades as we recalibrate our expectations.

It's like childhood, steadily burning through a roster of firsts. The more you repeat an experience, the less you feel its impact, almost as if your brain is gradually tuning out the world. Not today.

Sometimes you reach a point when you can't feel anything at all, just the wash from Typhoons ringing in your ears—until like Beethoven, you find yourself pounding the keys of your life, trying to make the ground thunder below your feet. It makes you remember to look around with fresh eyes and feel things just as powerfully as you did when you felt them for the first time.

I'm getting this feeling now. Adrenaline, a pirate's itch of feeling. The massive noise and huge speed required to jar and shake a new awakening. Eckhardt Tolle and the Power of Now.

Remember how big the world used to be? How wandering into the next neighbourhood felt like stepping into a foreign country.

It's like that now. We all know something big is about to happen yet none of us can predict it. We know it will be the same for the two police parked along the road.

It's Clare who sees it. "Is that a door?" she asks.

"No," says Chuck - "I think it's some kind of flat-looking self-propelled vehicle."

"A payload launched from the Mig," says Christina, "It went under the water but then resurfaced."

It's still a long way off, seemingly hovering above the water in the River Exe. But it is coming our way.

Suddenly Chuck realises, "It's a Ground Effect Vehicle - in other words, it's a target for something in orbit to shoot at!'"

We watch it as it slowly slithers to the bank of the Exe, continues through the grassy shoreline, past the police Land Rover and finally stops adjacent to the distant Assembly Hall and campus of Clyst Richard.

"They are going to use it to fire a weather weapon," says Chuck, looking around at us all, "Floor it Bigsy!"

With a slam, Bigsy boots the four wheels of our immense shed of a truck and we lurch forward. The self-propelled 'door' was going west, we are going east as fast as Bigsy can drive.

Then I hear a fierce splashing sound. It's water, dropped as if from buckets and hitting the ground and our truck.

"I've only once seen rain like this in Southern India," says Christina." *'Hani koodi halla'* (merger of raindrops makes a stream) says a Kannada proverb,"

ಕನ್ನಡ

"This is so severe, a monsoon," says Clare. We look around and see the water is washing the ground away. So powerful that the campus buildings appear to be sinking under water. In the distance, we can see cars swept away. I hope there is no-one inside. The police vehicle remains rooted to the spot, The electrical power will be out by now, yet Bigsy has driven us out of the danger zone.

I can't see the 'door' anymore; the Ground Effect

Vehicle has disappeared behind a deluge of rainfall. More than that, I can see the river is being convected in a circle to fall upon the remains of Clyst Richards.

"This is Biblical," says Chuck, "We never managed anything like this with iodide crystals, although I can recognise some of the signs."

"Less water where you were, in the deserts," says Christina, "Come to Britain for the best quality rainfall."

Suddenly it is over. There's lightning cracking and I can feel the animal sharpness of an electrostatic charge in the air, but we are suddenly surrounded by silence. It's the contrast between deep storm-rain and now, with quiet rivulets of water running away.

Then I see the Ground Effect Vehicle. It is making its way back into the river. This time it submerges and I assume its job is done. The police vehicle is still standing at the same spot, the two occupants seem very animated.

And we hear another sound. The old Spitfire runway is being used. I notice lights flick on and then, moments later see a small commercial twin-engined jet prepare for take-off.

"It's a Gulfstream, " says Christina, "lovely planes."

Chuck nods in agreement and we watch as the small blue and white jet builds speed and takes off, steeply to the east along the River Exe.

Then a whistling sound as the fighter planes we'd seen earlier fly back along the river. They travel faster than sound. This time I'm looking out for the twin tails of the Mig. By the time I realise it, the Gulfstream has vanished from sight.

"There!" says Christina, pointing skyward. The Mig is in the middle of the pack. As it flies over, I swear I saw it waggle its wings.

A subtle victory dance.

G-G-G-F. Dit-dit-dit-dah.

V for Victory.

Dots

The planes recede into so many dots. There are persistent contrails iced in the sky. The moment has passed. Time sweeps past, right where we sit in Bigsy's rented monster truck.

We all look at one another. We feel the inertia, sensing the present moment already turning into a memory, even as it's still happening. Somehow, we know we're going to remember this day. Some random detail that becomes a game changer.

You can almost feel the presence of your future self, looking back on this moment. Of course, by then it'll mean something very different. Maybe we'll cringe and laugh, or brim with pride, aching to return.

The police Land Rover is moving again, heading towards us.

So, we each look around the scene, trying to tell

in advance what this moment is going to mean. It's as if we're walking through the memory while it's still happening, feeling for all the world like a time traveller.

We notice how strange it all seems. All the quaint little gadgets and fads and slang terms that never made all that much sense. All the faces around, vibrant, fretting about the day's concerns, not yet realising that this world is already out of our hands and probably on a party jet heading for Moscow.

All of this will soon be swept away and replaced by something different. And yet nobody is stopping to take it all in or revel in the nostalgia of this world at this moment.

In a way, we really are time travellers, leaping into the future in little, tentative steps. A part of is like a kid stuck in a strange land without a map, with nothing to do but soak in the moment and take one last look before moving on. But another part of us is already old and looking back on things.

We are all two people, separated by an ocean of time. Part of you bursting to talk about what you saw. Part of you longing to tell you what it all means.

Exit

We've moved out of the hotel by the rugby field. We are back to the American-looking hotel at the airport. It's a partly a precaution from the extreme weather which hit the region yesterday. Plus, both Christina and Chuck said we needed to be somewhere different.

Bigsy didn't need any encouragement and so we throw our bags into the trunk of his large saloon car, leaving the enormous blue hired Mercedes SUV parked prominently at the front of the original hotel.

"I'll get it picked up in a couple of days, we should be out of here by then," says Bigsy.

I'm sure he is right.

DCI Morwen Penrose and DI Tristan Trewella have arranged to meet us. We suggest the busy microbrewery in central Dittlesham. It's a venue that has sprung up in an old fire station. But then, the old bank has become a pet shop and the other old bank is a tea and cakes cafe.

We've also invited Zoe Demelza and Li Mei, so with Clare, Bigsy, Chuck and Christina, we are able to take over a big corner table, waiting for Trewella and Penrose to arrive.

"Cask?" asks Bigsy, "Cask all around?"

We all nod - I realise that Devon has permeated our very existence.

"Eight pints of Exmouth," asks Bigsy. The barman smiles, " A gallon of Exmouth coming up!" he says, although Bigsy is already distracted by the pizza oven outside and I see he is calculating how many we all need.

Then, Penrose and Trewella arrive. They smile and it looks to me as if they are treating this as an off-duty visit.

"It's okay, we'll be getting a taxi back," says Clare, looking across the beers on the table.

"Same for us actually, " says Penrose, still smiling., "You guys - never a dull moment when you are around...We've had national television down to cover the freak weather and numerous reports of a spy plane in the Torbay Airshow."

"And it's curious how you ask us questions about Reverend Richards, just days before his entire campus is wiped out in a freak hurricane."

"And those reports of a jet plane taking off from that old Spitfire runway and disappearing with both of the Richards on board," says Trewella, "We think they hired a Gulfsteam jet from Exeter, moved it to the Clyst Richards property, and had it ready for a quick exit."

Penrose adds, "Don't underestimate it as a getaway vehicle - it has a 7,000-mile range and can fly at 600 miles per hour. Cape Town, Los Angeles, Moscow, Singapore - all within reach."

Clare summarises, "Richards was unwittingly doing something huge, bound in the motives of Brant. And Brant is still playing a vast and strategic game. Money is no object as it seeks power. Marie-Louise Deschanel and her murdered father François Deschanel discovered the route offering services to monied oligarchs. Our plan almost worked. Except it didn't.

We all look at one another. It's Zoe who speaks next.

"The Richards were on to a good thing. Well, an evil thing I suppose. Trafficking, Laundering, and beefing up the Brant Technology position. And we were so close...What happens next?"

Li Mei speaks, "Well guys, I think I may have the answer to that." She puts an iPhone on the table.

"It arrived this morning, courier delivery. The note said, 'run the Raven App'. I thought I'd wait until we were all together."

She starts the App.

“The clock is running,” says a small display on the screen.

“The clock is running and they got away,” adds Clare.

“Ominous,” says Bigsy.

Story

So, is life a story? A torrent of overlapping moments, rushing in no particular order. As the days flip past, it all happens far too quickly to absorb—a mess of seemingly random events.

Every once in a while, we look back and highlight certain memories as important and as turning points in the main plot. We trace each thread back to its origin, finding omens and ironies scattered along the way, until it all feels inevitable, even that life makes sense.

But then sometimes we look up and realise the life plot has a wiggle. We were following the arc of the story, but then a sudden twitch occurs and throws us into another derailment.

We keep finding ourselves immersed in sections we don't understand. Sometimes everything seems important, but then nothing does.

The line keeps changing depending on what we choose to highlight.

You look around and wonder, What kind of story is this? Truly epic? Or unwitting at the behest of others? Maybe making our own luck, Are we getting by on other people's indulgences, mistaking our own luck? Is it a romance, a tragedy, a travelogue, or just another cautionary tale?

As we stand back, we realise we may never know where this all is going. The only thing we know is that there's more to the story. Soon enough we'll notice, re-read parts, and look for clues. To learn that all along, we were supposed to choose our own adventure.

Dark

Join the escape flight of Brant in Dark. The next part of this Ed Adams series.

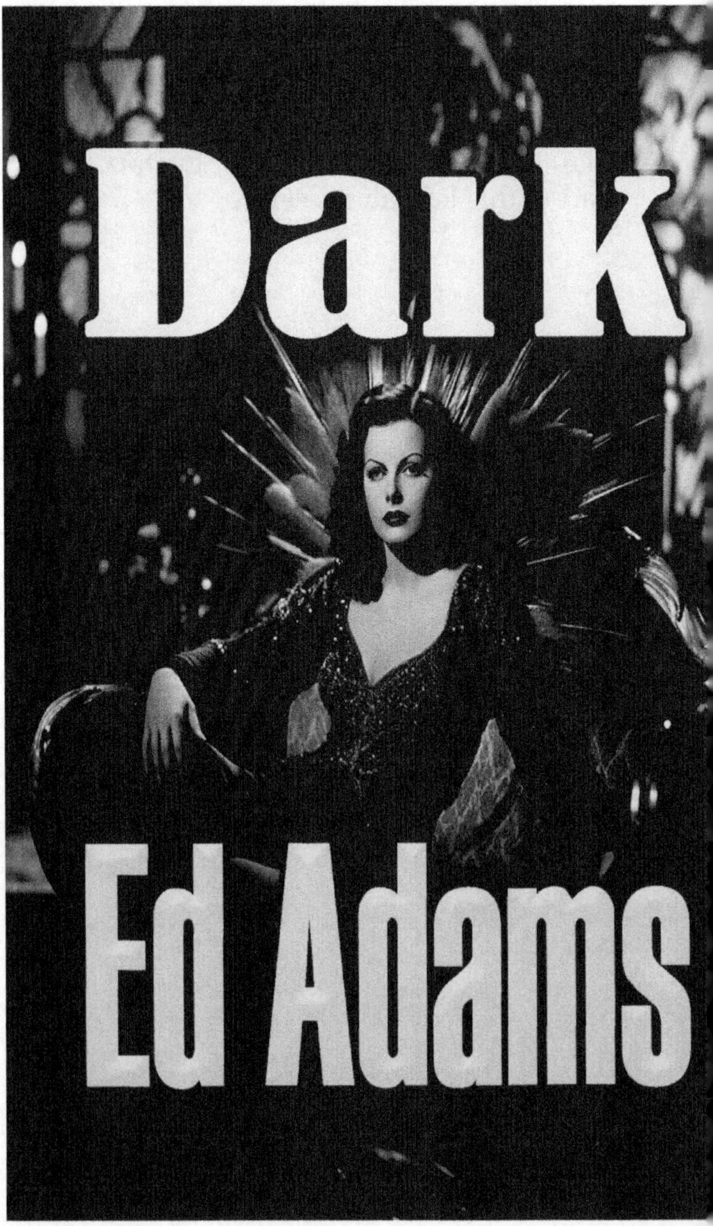
Dark
Ed Adams

Printed in Great Britain
by Amazon

42689656R00145